What happens in Oasis, stays at Oasis

A novella by DL Gallie
the Castaway Grove Collection, book #1

I0593930

Serena and her friends head off on a much needed, girls' only getaway to celebrate their graduation from college. They plan for a week of relaxation, dancing, cocktails, and tanning; but no guys.

That all changes when she spies sexy as sin Blake Bateman before their flight even leaves the ground.

Sparks fly.
Temperatures rise.
Desire builds.

Serena begins a week long fling with Blake, but when feelings start to develop, the lines become blurred.

Will it just be a holiday hook up?

Or did they find something special?

Something worth fighting for?

OASIS COPYRIGHT

All rights reserved. No part of this book may be reproduced or transmitted in any form, including electronic or mechanical, without written permission from the publisher, except in the case of brief quotations embodied in critical articles or reviews.

This is a work of fiction. Names, characters, businesses, places, events, and incidents are either the products of the author's imagination or used in a fictitious manner. Any resemblance to actual persons, living or dead, or actual events is purely coincidental. This book is licensed for your personal enjoyment only.

Published by DL Gallie Author

Published on 13th June 2017

Edited by Karen Hrdlicka, Barren Acres Editing

Cover Designed by Tash Drake, Outlined With Love Designs

Original formatting by Champagne Book Design

❀ Created with Vellum

The Castaway Grove Collection

Love has arrived in the grove

To friendships, old & new

CHAPTER 1

SERENA BATEMAN HAD JUST FINISHED COLLEGE AND BEFORE she started her dream job, as a junior editor at a leading women's magazine, she and her two best mates, Michele Hiddleston and Heather Downey, were taking a much-needed trip. They were off for a girls' only week to celebrate finishing college, to let loose one last time before settling down and becoming responsible adults. After living the student life for the past three years, they decided to splurge and head to Oasis; it was the hottest new resort to open in the beachside town of Castaways Grove, just a short flight from the mainland.

The girls were waiting in the departure lounge at the airport for their flight, each of them looking around and excited for the next seven days. Before long it was time to board their flight. "Ladies and gentleman, Flight OA727 to Castaways Grove is now boarding," was announced over the loud speaker.

"Let's board, bitches." Heather excitedly jumped up and squealed.

Michele and Serena both rolled their eyes. "Calm your tits, Heather. The plane won't leave without us," Michele stated, before she stood up to grab her carry-on bag and neck pillow.

"I'm just so fucking excited," Heather declared, as she continued to jump up and down on the spot, like a kid who had eaten four tonnes of M&M's—except the orange ones because they were eeww—and was on a total sugar high. "We have been slaves to the system for three years, three long fucking years, it's now OUR time. Before long, we will become real people and have to adult on a daily basis."

Michele replied, "You're right, Heather. This is going to be a fun-filled week o..."

Heather interrupted and eagerly shouted, "...of dancing, cocktails, tanning, and no boys!"

Michele and Serena both laughed at the no boys comment, not to high note themselves, but the three of them were pretty hot. The boys wouldn't be able to stay away, and from seeing who was on the flight with them, it would be hard for them to stay away as well.

"Okay, ladies, let's do this. The time for cocktails and tanning has finally arrived," Serena declared. The three of them finished collecting their belongings and then they lined up to board the plane. As they were walking towards the boarding gate, a guy caught Serena's eye, but she didn't get a chance to scope him out further because they were at the front of the boarding line.

The girls boarded the plane and made their way down the aisle to their seats in row seven; Serena was superstitious and always had to sit in a row with the number seven in it. They each took their seats: Heather by the window, Michele in the middle, and Serena on the aisle. Choosing to stow their bags under the seat in front for easy access, they settled in for the flight.

Heather was not so discreetly scoping out the talent, when the guy Serena noticed before boarding stopped next to her. He was at least six-foot tall, with a chiseled jaw, luscious lips, and defined shapely arms; he was an Adonis—holy fucking hotness, Batman. He stowed his bag in the overhead locker, Serena couldn't help but stare at his tight, perfect ass as he reached up. His two mates came up behind him and they were just as smokin' hot, this no boys rule just got really, really hard—pun intended...hopefully. He let his friends in before taking the aisle seat, directly across from Serena. Her eyes were glued to him. He hopped back up to grab something from his bag, and a not so quiet, appreciative moan erupted from Serena when she noticed his shirt ride up to expose his rock hard abs. He was wearing a tight, charcoal grey, V-neck shirt and khaki cargos that hugged his ass perfectly. All heads in the immediate vicinity snapped to look at her. Serena was embarrassed at her faux pas, her face turned beetroot red, so to cover her moan, she started to fake cough. Michele gently rubbed her back. "You right, sweet pea?"

"Yeah, just choked on my gum," Serena said, as she added another small fake cough, she rubbed her chest to keep up the charade.

Heather piped up, "You didn't have any gum."

Serena and Michele both stared daggers at Heather, while she looked at them confused. "Whaat?"

"Never mind," Michele and Serena said at the same time, before they both shouted, "Jinx," again at the same time.

They went to continue their jinx off like they always, when Heather jumped in, "Nope, nah, uh, not this shit again." That caused them to both start giggling. Serena began to snort laugh and that in turn set Michele off; the two of them were stuck in a laugh/snort cycle. Heather groaned, as she hated when that happened, but secretly she loved it.

Once the girls had stopped laughing, Michele leaned over and whispered, "You were totally checking out the hottie sitting over there." She flicked her head in the direction of Mr. Hot. "Weren't you?"

"Maybe," Serena quietly replied, as she leaned forward to grab something out of her bag. She shook her head and smirked to herself that her friend knew her too well and knew exactly whom she had been checking out. She turned her head slightly to perv when she noticed that Mr. Sex-on-a-Stick was staring at her. He smiled and winked at her before he turned his attention back towards his mates. His smile left Serena grinning to herself, her heart racing, butterflies fluttering in her tummy, and her panties damp. If he invoked these feelings from a smile, imagine what it would be like if he had actually spoken to her?

Serena sat back up and slid her iPad into the seat pocket when she felt his gaze upon her again. From across the aisle, she heard a deep, gravely, sexy voice that caused her insides to stir, growl, "Hey."

With just one word, Serena melted and was totally smitten. When she turned her head, she saw that Mr. Sex-on-a-Stick was staring intently at her and he was smiling. Serena found herself grinning back at him. "Hey, yourself," she casually replied, twisting her body so she was facing him. She leaned across the aisle and stretched out her hand. "I'm Serena Bateman."

As he took her offered hand in his, an electric shock zapped them; they both jolted but neither let go. They were locked in a handshake across the aisle, stopping traffic, but they were oblivious to everyone around them. Serena had never felt an instant connection like that before; she was nervous and excited all at the same time. They were brought back to reality by a throat clearing and the angry tapping of a foot. They looked up, to be met with the glare of a pissed off, short, redheaded dude. "If you two are finished eye fucking each other, can you let me get past?" They both let go and immediately they felt the loss. As the grumpy asshole passed, he muttered under his breath, "And don't even think about fucking in the bathroom."

They both chuckled, before he whispered to Serena, "Someone clearly needs to get laid." They both burst out laughing and continued to gaze at each other across the aisle. Serena found herself snort laughing, again, but around Mr. Hottie she wasn't embarrassed. When she stopped laughing, he said, "Pleasure to meet you, Serena, I'm Blake Kelton. It was nice to piss someone off with you."

"The pleasure was all mine, maybe we can do it again sometime." Serena winked at Blake before she shuffled around in her seat. From her peripheral vision she noticed that both Michele and Heather were staring at her, she turned to face them and their eyebrows were raised. "Whaaaat?" Serena asked.

"Don't whaat us, missy. NO BOYS ALLOWED," Heather deadpanned.

"Says the girl who was scoping out the talent as soon as we arrived, and when we checked in, while waiting to board, and as soon as we sat down," Serena scoffed.

"Scoping and eye fucking are two completely different things," she retorted.

"Now, now, girls," Michele interjected. "Listen, we are here for fun and flirting is fun, so suck it, princess." She turned to Serena and added, "But that's all it will be, flirting only."

Serena noticed however that Michele was not looking at her. Her eyes were locked on the blue-eyed, blond-haired hottie, sitting in the middle, next to Blake.

Their no boys rule was proving difficult...for all...and they hadn't even taken off yet.

CHAPTER 2

BLAKE, TOM, AND ROBERT WERE LOOKING FORWARD TO THEIR boys' week away. They had been doing an annual trip since they met, freshman year at college, and continued the tradition after they entered the workforce. This year, however, was the first time that they were going to a beachside resort. Normally, it was pretty laid back and cruisy: camping, beers, and fishing in the woods, just the three of them.

Due to Tom's eagerness and slight—secret code for borderline needs to be instutionalised—OCD, they arrived at the airport early, super-duper early. They were waiting in the departure lounge, when Blake noticed an absolutely gorgeous, golden-haired beauty with two other girls. Her beauty mesmerised him, he only had eyes for her. He discreetly watched her with her friends, and the first thing he noticed was her smile. When she smiled, her whole face lit up; he found himself also grinning and her laugh was magical…even with the snorting.

Blake vaguely listened to the conversation between Tom and Robert but his mind and eyes kept drifting; never had a girl entranced him like this. It was as if she'd cast a spell over him, he was besotted, almost helpless when it came to her. Robert busted Blake staring and his eyes glanced around the lounge when he noticed a brunette excitedly jumping up and down. He did a double take; she was absolutely drop-dead fucking gorgeous. He then noticed the chick next to her and he knew that Blake was smitten. Like hawks, the two of them watched the girls gather their belongings when the boarding call was announced.

As luck would have it, the three sexy sirens were also on the same flight to Castaways Grove. Blake watched her walk towards the gate and he decided in that moment to turn their threesome into a six-some. It was perfect; three of them, three girls, a winning combination…this getaway just went from awesome to fucking amazeballs and they hadn't even departed yet.

Tom draped his arm over Blake and Robert's shoulders; oblivious to them checking out the girls and Blake's new plan. "Let's go, assholes. Oasis is awaiting."

"Fuck yeah," Blake replied, his eyes still glued to the golden-haired angel.

While Robert declared, "Fuckin' oath, let's make this getaway our bitch, motherfuckers."

The three of them laughed and joked as they lined up, but Blake's eyes were steadfastly locked on Goldilocks, who was only a few people ahead of them. He watched her every move and was captivated by the way her ass swayed as she ambled down the gangway. Her white skirt hugged her womanly curves and her navy halter show-cased her shoulders. His eyes drifted down to her ass, again, and he intently watched as it swished from side to side with each step that she took up the plane aisle. Stopping suddenly, she allowed her friends to go ahead of her; she was only three people in front of him. His eyes were locked on the back of her head and he bumped into Tom, who turned and gave him a 'what the fuck' look. Blake just shrugged his shoulders in a 'oops, sorry, get over it' kind of way.

Once again, his eyes drifted ahead and Blake smiled when he realised that she would be sitting in the row across from him. He inwardly high-fived himself and thanked the gods for bringing them closer together...he was suddenly excited for the eight hour flight ahead of him.

Tom and Robert shuffled into their seats, with Tom immediately grumbling about the lack of legroom, but Blake and Robert ignored him, not wanting to encourage him. At six-foot-two, Tom was always squished and there-fore complaining. Blake continued to stare at her; she turned her head and totally busted him perving on her. She didn't seem annoyed, and that shocked him, so he smiled back; her face lit up, highlighting the green of her eyes and the silkiness of her skin. And in the blink of an eye, she had turned her attention back to her friends. Before his brain caught up, he said "hey!" *What the fuck, you dickhead*, he thought to himself while he waited for her reaction. Her head turned back towards him and she eyed him across the aisle, before she grinned cheekily. Blake imagined himself leaning over, gripping her cheeks and kissing her senseless. Instead, he shook her outstretched hand and tried to act like the nice, responsible gentleman that Granny raised him to be...and in the process, they managed to piss off a little, fat, redheaded leprechaun, who clearly needed to get his cock sucked.

After he introduced himself, Blake turned his attention back towards Tom and Robert. *Always leave them wanting more*, he thought to himself as he focused on the conversation going on between his friends, but it was hard for him to concentrate—his thoughts kept wandering to the golden-haired beauty, who sat a few meters from him. It seemed that Tom's previous outburst was long forgotten and his focus was then turned to the flight's open bar. Blake vaguely listened to Tom blabber on about the different activities available at Oasis and how excited he was that the flight had original chips, because original chips were the best flavour and blah blah blah. However, at that moment, all he could think about was laying on the beach with Serena, his body cocooning hers. Their tongues wrestling together before he stripped off her bikini and he sank himself balls-deep into her wet and waiting pussy.

Fuck, this is going to be one long-ass flight.

CHAPTER 3

THE PLANE FINALLY TOUCHED DOWN AND SERENA WAS already dreading the return trip home. Michele did not stop talking for the entire flight; eight fracken hours, Serena didn't get to read one word of her book or get a nap in. Thank God there was free wine, lots of Sav Blanc was consumed on that flight and surprisingly, she wasn't as pissed as she thought she'd be. Heather had two vodkas and fell straight to sleep…snoring loudly at times and talking about gummy bear wrestling and cheering on the orange one. Michele and Serena laughed at that, considering her aversion to all things orange.

Heather woke up when the plane commenced its descent into paradise. Her head was glued to the window and she gave Michele and Serena a running commentary of the view. "Fuck me, the water is amazing, it's blue-blue, like Tiffany's blue, and the sand is so white and the trees are green, like really green."

Michele and Serena glanced at one another and were trying their hardest to contain their laughter, but after the third description of the trees, it was too much. They both burst out laughing. Serena, through snorts, managed to say, "Heather, honey, you definitely are no David Attenborough with your commentary."

"Pfft, whatevs. When he passes, God rest his soul, they will be calling me up to take his place as the next documentary commentator extraordinaire." She looked towards Michele and Serena, and in her best Attenborough voice, she responded with, "And here we have three, smokin' hot young ladies, about to embark on the adventure of a lifetime." Even she couldn't keep her face straight that time, and the three of them laughed and laughed as the plane landed in paradise.

Serena waited until the aisle ahead was clear to get off the plane, much to Heather's disgust; what's the point in standing and being crushed when you can sit and take your time without the pushing and shoving—people can be assholes when they fly…and in general. She constantly complained of being cramped from sitting near the window and wanting to get out. Michele finally had enough and snapped, "Shut it, Heather. You chose the window seat, so suck it up, princess." Immediately she apologised for being rude, like always. Michele was super nice and hated hurting peoples' feelings. Serena loved to watch her let loose on someone, only to instantly turn around and apologise for being rude. That trait was one of the many things that Serena loved about Michele.

Walking through the tin shed that was Castaways Grove's airport, the three girls apprehensively looked around and started to wonder if maybe they had booked into Shitsville. After clearing customs, they collected their bags, and made their way to the shuttle waiting to take them to Oasis. Serena noticed that Blake was also in the same shuttle line, and she really hoped that he and his friends were heading to Oasis with them.

The shuttle was jam-packed until the first resort stop; Serena observed that Blake and his friends didn't get off. Silently, she thanked her lucky stars and grinned like the Cheshire cat...it seemed like he was also going to Oasis. Both Michele and Heather noticed her dreamily grinning and looked at her questioningly. "Ladies, we are finally on our way to Oasis. I'm so bloody excited. As soon as we check in, it's on with my kini, and then I'm finding a cabana, which will be mine for the next week. Then I'm going to drink mojitos all afternoon until I can't stand up. And then I'm going to do it all again the tomorrow."

Heather's face broke out into a huge smile and she loudly declared, "Fuck yeah, let's do this, bitches."

The girls garnered a few odds looks from those also on the shuttle, but the three sinfully sexy men from the plane seemed to be amused, and they couldn't stop staring at each other.

Forty-five minutes later, the minibus finally pulled up at Oasis, and for the first time since they left, Michele was speechless...and quiet. This resort was the epitome of paradise: pure white sandy beaches lined with coconut trees, azure blue water lapping at the shore. At the water's edge, catamarans, jet-skis, and canoes were parked up, and cabanas were positioned along the beach for as far as they eye could see. The resort itself was stunning; there were three main buildings that wrapped around the pool. The buildings were simple yet beachy, each with three floors. The far building housed the restaurant and bar on the ground floor and the spa on the top floor at the end, overlooking the beach. The main pool was a lagoon style, complete with a thatched roof swim-up bar, which was a miniature version of the beachfront bar, and the second pool was located behind reception. It was much smaller but it had a waterslide and outdoor spa...this place was an adults-only paradise. "Fuck me!" the three of them all shrieked at once; causing them to break out in laughter, again garnering looks from the other guests.

"We are literally in paradise," Michele said, as her eyes darted around the place, taking the scenery in. Serena followed Michele's line of sight and noticed that she was staring and seductively smiling at Blake's blond friend and not taking in the magnificence that was Oasis...the little minx Serena thought. Then she had an epiphany, three plus three equals an awesome time at Oasis.

"This place is more beautiful than you described, Heather," Serena mocked, as she eyed up the cabanas. "That cabana at the end there totally has my name on it, and those three seats there," pointing to the swim-up bar, "are reserved for us."

Heather poked her tongue at Serena's comment before she added, "You're not wrong, S. It looked amazing from above, but on the ground, fuck me, this is, umm, yeah, wow." Looking around, Heather's eyes locked with a brown-haired guy, who was chatting with his friends, the same guys sitting across from them on the plane. Unashamedly, Heather winked at him, before she linked arms with Michele and Serena. "Let's get checked in and let the chilaxation begin."

"Best decision you have ever had, Heather," Michele said, as the three of them headed into reception. After checking in, they made their way to the elevators and headed up to their room to unpack and change.

CHAPTER 4

LUCK SEEMED TO BE FOLLOWING BLAKE, TOM, AND ROBERT when it came to the three sexy sirens from the airport. Not only were they all on the same flight, AND sitting next to one another, BUT there was also a high probability that they were staying at Oasis. Blake watched them intently on the shuttle trip, they interacted just like he did with the guys; they were obviously close. When the shuttle pulled up at the first resort, he held his breath in hope that they were heading to the same place. He sighed in relief when they didn't get off. For the rest of the trip, he continued to listen to them—not in a stalkerlike way though. It was hard not to laugh along with them, it seemed like they were great friends; much like him and the guys.

The shuttle finally arrived at Oasis, and while they

were waiting for their bags to be unloaded, Blake looked towards the guys and stated, "This decision to swap from camping to a beach resort was a fucking great idea."

Tom looked towards him, with a smug grin, and retorted, "You sure have changed your tune; for weeks now you have bitched and moaned about this like a fucking girl, ever since Robert and I suggested and booked something different. Why the sudden change?"

"Well, have you looked at this place?" He glanced around, but his eyes locked on Serena's as he eagerly replied, "This place is stunning." With a huge smile on his face, and a hard-on from the beauty of Serena that was becoming extremely painful.

"Yeah, it's this place and not some hot blonde piece of ass that has you changing your mind," Robert scoffed.

"No idea what you're talking about, asshole." But as he said that, his eyes were still glued to Serena and he couldn't help but smirk...he hated it when Robert was right but at that moment, he really didn't care. He just wanted a chance to get to know Serena.

"Fuck off you don't, but I don't care what caused you to change your tune. I'm ready to sit at the swim-up bar and get rip roaring shit-faced, and then tomorrow, I'm gonna to do it all over again," Tom declared. "Now let's get checked in and go get our drink on,"

"You had me at shit-faced." Robert replied, before he grabbed his bag and headed towards check-in.

The guys lined up and ahead of them were the three girls. Blake watched Serena's every move; he was capti-vated by her and was hoping like hell that he got a chance to get to know her while at Oasis. Eavesdropping on the girls, he heard that they were in room fifty-two on the top floor, and he secretly hoped that their room was nearby.

His eyes followed as the three girls headed left, towards their room. The guys checked-in and finally it looked like their luck had run out, they were in room 156…on the opposite side of the resort to the girls.

Opening the door to their room, the three of them were left open-mouthed and shocked. This place was bigger than they could have imagined and much more opulent then a tent. Walking into the room, it opened into a large, spacious, combined lounge-dining area with a balcony, to the left a simple kitchen and the master bedroom. To the right were the other two bedrooms and main bathroom.

Immediately, Blake yelled, "Dibs, master is mine!"

Tom and Robert both groaned before Tom bellowed. "Dibs on front room!"

"Fuck off, why do I get the shitty room?" Robert complained.

"Not our fault you're slow." Blake came back with, before he and Tom laughed as they each headed to their respective rooms. Robert continued to grumble about getting the shitty back bedroom as he headed towards his room. His attitude soon changed when he realised his room had its own balcony, too. "Ha-ha, fuckers, my room has a balcony overlooking…" Opening the curtains, he cussed, "Fuck, a view of the dumpsters."

Tom and Blake both laughed harder but neither of them said anything further on the matter; they didn't want to enrage the beast. Robert could get fired up pretty quickly and they wanted to have a fun, relaxing getaway.

Blake yelled, "Ten minutes, assholes, and then it's beer o'clock and since I got the master room, the first round is on me."

Robert yelled back, "Now you're talking," slamming his bedroom door.

Blake shook his head at Robert's change of attitude but beer does fix everything; fortunately after all these year, he knew exactly how to calm him down...beer or boobs worked every time. He looked around his room and smiled, it had a massive king-sized bed, complete with matching side tables. There was also a timber dresser on the wall by the entry to the ensuite, not that he'd be using it, as he never unpacked when away. As he walked towards the balcony, he thought to himself that it was not a bad place to call home for the next seven days. He pulled back the curtains, unlocked the slider, and stepped outside. Breathing in the fresh beach air, he closed his eyes and looked up towards the sky, soaking in the sunlight and atmosphere. Opening his eyes again, the first thing he noticed was Serena, in her room, which was directly opposite his. Her curtains were open and he couldn't help but stare. Standing there, Blake watched, his eyes locked on her and only her; he was mesmerised by her movements, her beauty, and her grace. She spun around and bent over, giving him an eyeful of ass, not that he minded. After digging around in her suitcase, she stood back up. Her delicate fingers, hooked into the top of her skirt and she shimmied it down and over her hips. She then grabbed the hem of her halter-top and lifted it over her head, leaving her in her bra and panties; she was the complete package.

Blake knew it was wrong to stare and watch her change, and that he should turn away, but he was frozen, his eyes were solely focused on Serena. She removed her bra and pulled her panties down her legs, standing naked in front of him, sort of. Once again his cock was rock hard at the sight before him. Serena was stunning: long lean legs, firm ass, perfect tits, and taut pink nipples. He groaned when she leaned over to pick up her bikini. She stepped into the bottoms before slipping the top over her head, tying the top at her neck. When she was redressed, she looked up and her eyes locked with Blake's. They stared at one another for a few moments before she quickly shut the curtains, obviously in embarrassment. Her sudden movement snapped Blake back to reality. He shook his head and mumbled, "Fuck," to himself as he went back inside with a raging hard-on and feeling regretful. He felt like an ass for watching her getting changed... but not that much because she had a smoking hot body and tits to die for.

CHAPTER 5

SERENA HAD JUST FINISHED TYING HER BIKINI TOP WHEN SHE looked up and noticed a guy on the balcony across from her...staring into her room...watching her intently. "Fuck!" she screeched to the room before she quickly closed the curtains, totally embarrassed that someone had just watched her get changed. She hoped that he only appeared once her bikini was on, but she highly doubted that...not with her luck.

"What's wrong, babes?" Michele asked as she walked into Serena's room, tying her sarong around her waist.

"Umm, I think I just flashed a guy as I got changed."

Michele burst out laughing. "Only you could do that within the first hour of arriving." She sat on the end of the bed and handed Serena her cover-up, "This is pretty. Was he at least hot?" She winked as she said it.

"Thanks. And I don't know, I didn't look. I just closed the curtains and slowly died inside."

"Ohh, babe, I'm sorry, but seriously that's the funniest shit ever. If he was hot, you should have given him a free show." She raised her eyebrows in a sexy, seductive way before she stood up, bent down, and flicked her head and hair up, bringing out her inner stripper, just as Heather walked in. Heather stood behind Michele, and proceeded to mimic slapping her ass and grinding into her.

"Wow, what did I miss? And whose become a stripper?"

"Our girl, here, she thinks she gave some guy across the resort an unintentional strip show," Michele said, as she sat back on the bed and pointed out the door.

"Was he hot?" Heather asked as she took a sip of water from her bottle.

"As I told Misty Bloodlust here, I was too embarrassed and are you drinking water? I'm disappointed, Heather." She pointed to the dresser and a glass of wine.

Heather laughed as she grabbed the wine, "Cheers." Raising it up in a silent salute, before she took a sip. Placing it back on the dresser, she headed over to the curtains, "Misty Bloodlust, I love that." She pulled the curtains open again and stepped outside.

"That name needs to stop," Michele said as she joined Heather outside.

"No way, Misty," Heather said, and she began to sway her hips against the railing.

Serena hesitantly stepped out to join them and giggled at Heather's gyrating. Her eyes darted across to the other building and noticed that there was no one on their balconies. Subconsciously she was searching for Blake but mostly hoping that she didn't run into her pervert again.

Heather was still dancing and singing to herself as Serena and Michele headed back inside, leaving her to it. Michele turned to close and lock the slider before she smirked at Heather and closed the curtains. Serena quickly raced into the lounge to lock that door too, but Heather was too fast and made it inside before they could lock her out. "You're both bitches," Heather snarled as Michele and Serena both laughed.

"But you love us anyways," Serena said, linking her arm with Heather's. "Now, let's go chillax by the pool and drink cocktails out of coconuts and pineapples AND to sweeten the deal, the first jug of mojitos is on me."

"Well, if you insist," Heather said, winking, linking her arm with Michele. "Come on, Misty, it's time to get our drink on."

Giggling, the three girls grabbed their beach bags and headed down to the pool for an unforgettable afternoon of fun, sun, sand, and cocktails.

CHAPTER 6

SITTING ON THE END OF THE BED, BLAKE FLOPPED BACK AND whispered, "Fuuuuck." He wanted to get to know Serena, but he didn't think that would happen due to the incident that just happened. It would seem to her that he was a creeper and Blake was far from a creeper... now if it was Robert, they'd definitely pop him into the category of creeper...with a big heart...and a soft side.

Jumping up, Blake headed into the ensuite; he pulled down his pants, gripped his rock hard cock and began stroking. Resting the other hand on the counter, he closed his eyes and imagined it was Serena's hand pumping up and down. It didn't take long before Blake exploded, coming all over his hand, letting out a grunt as he did so. Feeling relieved after flogging off, he washed up, changed into his boardies, and headed out into the lounge room.

Blake paused midstep when he noticed that both Tom and Robert had smug looks in their faces. "What?" he deadpanned.

"Floggy McFloggerson is in da house," Robert said, while he mimicked the wanking motion.

Tom fell back on the couch and laughed, "Dude, we've been here for ten minutes and your already spanking the monkey. What's with that?"

"Fuck off, assholes, if I wanna wank, I'll wank. Now, let's go sit at the swim-up bar and get shit-faced."

"Sounds like a plan but first, wash your wanky hands again." Robert scrunched his nose in disgust. "I don't want to be drinking Blake's lil' swimmers."

Blake flipped Robert off, grabbed his cap, and *Oakleys* off the table and stormed out of the room, slamming the door behind him.

Tom looked over to Robert and shrugged. "Looks like that wank didn't relax him, maybe a few beers will do that."

"I like that plan, but can we stop talking about Blake's tiny cock and recent wankfest? There are other things I would rather be thinking about, and they don't have dicks or balls."

Tom shook his head and ignored Robert; he left the room to join Blake. He found Blake waiting at the lifts, Tom slapped his back. "Dude, what's up your ass?"

"Nothing, I'm fine," Blake shortly replied.

"Fine, my ass. Dude, we are in paradise and you're all tense and acting like Robert." Blake snapped his head towards Tom. "Yep, you're being a Robert-hole. Now, what's crawled up your ass? You were on cloud nine before your wank and now you're a miserable, cranky fucker."

"I've blown my chance with her," he replied dejectedly.

"Who? The smokin' blonde hottie?" Tom enquired.

He nodded his head and smiled as he said her name, "Serena."

"What happened?" Tom asked, completely confused at this point.

"Well, I kinda sorta watched her getting changed. I just stood there, staring like a perverted freak and she saw me. Now she's going to think I'm a creeper."

"She won't think that, she will probably just laugh about, and if not, we'll get Robert to do some stupid shit and all will be forgotten." Tom paused and then added, "You really like this girl, don't you?"

"Yeah, I do and it's totally, fucking crazy. We've said like twelve words to one another, but I'm drawn to her like a moth to a flame. What the fuck is that all about?"

"You're asking the wrong person, dude, but my advice, for what it's worth, have a fun sexy fling in Oasis, and don't let an unintentional strip show ruin that."

Just as the lift doors opened, they heard Robert from behind. "Strip show, fuck yeah." Tom and Blake ignored him and climbed into the lift as Robert jogged towards them. Tom repeatedly punched the close doors button and they shut right before Robert could get in.

"Fuckers." They heard him growl just as the lift doors closed.

"He's gonna be pissed at us for that," Tom said.

Blake just shrugged his shoulders. "We'll buy him a beer and all will be forgiven."

"That's true. Now, let's go get fuckin' shit-faced as you

suggested after your wank. And maybe we can come up with a way for you to win over your girl."

"Fucking hell, I'm never going to live that down, am I?"

"Not until Robert does something stupid…so not long at all."

Tom and Blake both laughed. The lift doors opened and they stepped out to be met by a huffing, puffing Robert. "You two are fuckers, big ones. Now, let's go get shit-faced."

The three of them silently walked towards the pool area. Blake hoped he hadn't blown his chance with Serena, Tom prayed he didn't get sunburned, and Robert thought about beer and boobs.

The sun was high in the sky and it was perfect swimming, tanning, and drinking weather. They placed their belongings on three loungers and dived into the pool, the water was perfect. Robert was the first one at the bar— surprise, surprise—he ordered three beers. Tom and Blake joined him and he handed out the drinks. "Cheers, motherfuckers," Robert declared.

"Cheers," Tom and Blake said in return, clinking their plastic mugs together before chugging back their first beer. Robert ordered another round of drinks, as they each took a seat around the bar, and fell into their normal mockery and shenanigans; Blake's wank soon forgotten.

On their third beer, Tom nudged Blake and he looked up to where Tom was nodding subtly with his head. The vision before them was magnificent; Serena and her friends were walking towards the pool area, the three of them glowing like angels in the midday sun. Every male, and a few females, in the pool area were staring at the girls; they were fucking stunning.

Everything and everyone around Blake faded away; his eyes were locked on Serena and Serena only. She was wearing a white see-through thingy that stopped mid-thigh over her black bikini; she was breathtakingly beautiful and more gorgeous than he remembered. Bending over, she placed her things on the chair next to Blake's, before straightening up to remove her shirt thingy. Blake's eyes were fused on Serena and her movements. He watched as her hands grabbed the hem of her cover-up and she slowly lifted it up her tanned, toned legs, up her tight tummy, over her fantastic tits, and over her head. Throwing it on the chair, she bent down and grabbed something out of her bag. Blake groaned when she bent over, Tom scoffed but his eyes were glued to Serena's friend.

Standing back up, she shook out her hair before grabbing the sunscreen spray and lathering up. Blake's eyes watched as she rubbed the lotion all over her body—never had he been so turned on as he had been in the moment as he watched her apply it. She then walked over to the pool and sat on the edge, her legs dangling in the water. Leaning back on her arms, she looked towards the heavens and thrust her gorgeous tits in the air. Blake's cock began to twinge and he quietly groaned; again. Never in his whole twenty-five years had any woman captivated him like Serena had, he would make it his mission to get to know her while at Oasis.

His eyes were riveted to Serena; everyone else in the vicinity didn't matter or count. She removed her sunnies and placed them on the edge before she slipped into the water. Taking a deep breath, she ducked under and when she emerged, water cascaded down her shoulders and over her breasts. With her back to him, she slipped her sunnies back on, leaned against the edge, and began to chat with her friends.

Blake was hypnotised by her actions, his cock was suddenly standing to attention, and he was happy to have the water shielding it from view. Her laugh echoed across the pool and Blake smiled. He would have loved nothing more than for her to be laughing with him.

The next thing Blake knew, Serena and her friends were swimming towards them; well, they were probably heading over to the swim-up bar, but he hoped it was towards him. Serena dived under the water for the last few meters to the bar. She surfaced in front of Blake; water teeming down her shoulders, and once again, Blake's eyes followed the water droplets. He realised that he was staring at her tits, thankful for his sunnies masking his eyes and for the pool water hiding his erection.

"Hey, Blake," Serena said, as she sat on the stool next to him.

"Hey," he replied, all of a sudden he was nervous and couldn't string a sentence together. Her voice was angelic and it sent shockwaves straight to his cock.

"Blake, these are my friends, Heather Downey and Michele Hiddleston," Serena said, pointing to her friends, and they waved at him.

He managed a wave back. "Hey! This is Tom Stratton," he pointed behind him, "And that douche over there is Robert Young." Tom waved and Robert flipped Blake off before taking the seat next to Heather, sitting dangerously close to her and putting on his smooth moves…Heather seemed to melt into him, obviously smitten.

"Can I buy you ladies a drink?" Robert asked, nicely. He winked seductively at Heather as he signaled for the bartender.

"Thanks," Michele said, not looking at Robert, her eyes were locked on Tom's. Heather nodded, her attention solely on Robert. Serena nodded and replied, "Three mojito's would be great, thanks, Robert."

Blake's eyes were gazing at Serena, and even though she was wearing her sunnies, he was pretty sure that her eyes were on him, too. The bartender came over and Robert ordered the girls a round of mojitos and three more beers for himself and the guys. AND for once, Robert came to the party and held up his end of the deal, he actually paid for the round of drinks...he shocked both Tom and Blake with that.

The six of them fell into easy conversation and shared many drinks, laughs, and stories over the course of the afternoon. As more and more drinks were consumed, the air became thick with lust and their inhibitions lowered.

CHAPTER 7

THE SUN WAS BEGINNING TO SET; THE SKY WAS A FIERY RED, mixed with orange, pink, and purple. Even though the sun was setting, it was still stifling hot...and not from the weather. The group had separated into pairs. Robert and Heather were doing shots together, down at the beachfront bar. Michele and Tom were sitting on the sun lounges, deep in conversation sharing a bottle of wine; while Serena and Blake were still at the swim-up bar drinking mojitos and beer, inching closer and closer together. Their legs were precariously close; Blake casually placed his palm on Serena's thigh and lazily drew circles and figures of eight with his fingertips, staring intently at her. The highly charged moment was interrupted by a large group, jumping into the pool and splashing around, pushing their way to the bar; effectively dousing the burning flames. Blake leaned over and whispered, "Want to go for a walk along the beach? Just the two of us?"

Serena licked her lips and eagerly nodded. "Mmhmm."

Blake stood up and put his hand out for Serena to take. She placed her hand in his, creating a spark as they laced their fingers together. Standing up, they waded to the edge and climbed out. Being a gentleman, Blake let Serena go first, but in all honesty, it was so he could stare at her sexy ass; bad idea, his cock started to spasm. After he climbed out, he discreetly adjusted himself as he slipped on his flip flops. Serena grabbed her cover-up and slipped it over her head, she then bent over to put her flip flops on. Blake groaned when she covered her sexy body but when she grabbed his hand, once again lacing their fingers, he smiled.

Together they made their way down to the beach, passing Heather and Robert. They were doing body tequila shots...Robert was currently licking salt off her neck, and she held a wedge of lime between her lips. After sinking back the shot, he sucked the lime from Heather's lips and it turned into a heated X-rated kiss. Serena blushed at watching her friend make out like that and quickly turned her focus towards Blake, dragging him away from the beachfront bar and live-action tequila porn.

They walked hand-in-hand, in comfortable silence along the shoreline, taking in the scenic view before them. They were both nervous to be alone around each other in such a romantic setting. Eventually, they reached the end of the private beach so Serena sat down in the sand, effectively pulling Blake down with her, as their hands were still laced together. He landed with a thud next to her. "Oh My God, I'm so sorry, Blake," she said, as she rubbed his arm.

"It's fine. Just wasn't expecting to be pulled."

Serena's cheeks turned pink, her eyes drifted down to his crotch, her mind immediately going to the gutter at the mention of pulled. Blake reached out and lifted her chin. "Eyes up here, gorgeous." She giggled and her cheeks darkened further, she lowered her gaze to her hands in her lap.

"Sorry, I, ahh…"

"It okay, it's only fair you look, since I've seen you naked."

Her head snapped up towards him. "That was you?" she nervously asked.

Blake wasn't sure if Serena was relieved or pissed off that it was him, so he hesitantly nodded his head up and down.

After what felt like an eternity, she finally said, "Ohh, thank God it was you. I was afraid I'd done a striptease for some skeezy freak."

Relieved at her answer, he said, "I'm so sorry, Serena. I knew I should have looked away, but when I saw it was you, I couldn't. It was like I was in a trance, and then when you saw me staring, I thought you'd hate me and think I was a creeper."

"I was embarrassed beyond belief, but to be honest," she swallowed deeply and glanced over at Blake, "I'm glad it was you." Feeling brave and bold, Serena grabbed the hem of her cover-up and lifted it over her head. Blake's eyes immediately roamed over her body. Eventually, his eyes made their way to her face, and he was staring into

Serena's sparkling emerald eyes. A force beyond his control over took his body and he placed his hand behind Serena's head and pulled her towards him; his lips crashed against hers. His tongue seeking access, she opened slightly and Blake plunged his tongue into her mouth. Pulling her closer, he lifted her so she was straddling his lap. Wrapping her arms tightly around his neck, she pressed her breasts into his bare muscular chest. She began to circle her hips on Blake's growing cock, the only thing separating them was her barely there bikini bottom and his boardies. They moaned into each other's mouths as their kiss deepened and they lost themselves in one another.

Blake leaned back and lay down in the sand, bringing Serena with him, before he flipped her onto her back, encasing her within his arms. Resting on his elbows so as to not crush her, she felt his arm muscles flex and she moaned into his mouth. Their tongues continued their erotic dance together. His palm cupped her left breast, gently massaging it before freeing it from the tiny material covering it. He rolled her nipple between his thumb and forefinger, slightly pinching it. She arched her back and ground herself up and into his pelvis. Breaking the kiss, Blake nipped and sucked down her neck, before taking her erect nipple into his mouth, gently biting down on the taut peak as he sucked tenderly. Letting it pop back out, he moved over to her other breast. Sucking it through the material while continuing to massage the first. Serena lifted her hips and continued to grind into his cock. She wrapped her legs around his thighs, pulling him closer to her.

The moment was interrupted when two guys, walking along the beach, whistled and shouted, "He's gonna fuck her on the beach!" and "Ohh yeah, uh ha. Fuck her hard, dude!"

Blake quickly covered her exposed breast, giving it a slight squeeze as he gazed deep into Serena's eyes. Her cheeks were once again a deep shade of embarrassed pink but her eyes were full of lust and want. Forgetting about their audience, he leaned back down and kissed her deeply, rolling her again so she was on top, straddling him. They kissed for a few moments before Serena broke the connection and whispered, "I think we should take a dip and cool off." She sat back on her heels over his thighs.

"You go and I'll catch up." Serena looked inquisitively at him. He glanced down to his obviously tented boardies. She looked up and down the beach before she seductively whispered. "It's just us, now, come on."

She tugged on his hand, and she managed to pull him up before he quickly grabbed her around her thighs and threw her over his shoulder, making a beeline for the water. Serena was laughing, squealing, and wriggling in his arms, playfully swatting his ass. When Blake was in the water at waist height, he dove in, dunking them both. When they both resurfaced, Serena was laughing. *She has the most magical laugh,* Blake thought to himself, as she shoved him in the chest before trying to dunk him.

He gripped her by the hips and pulled her towards him; she wrapped her legs around his waist, draping her arms over his shoulders, and kissed him. Her tongue plunged into his mouth, and he eagerly welcomed the intrusion. Their teeth bumping in a heat-filled rough kiss.

Serena shamelessly ground herself on him again. Blake lowered his hand under the water and began to rub her clit through her bikini bottoms, as he continued to kiss her passionately. Serena untied her bikini bottom on one side, giving Blake easy and full access. Within seconds, his finger was sliding up and down her slit, rubbing circles on her pulsating clit. Circling her hips, she unashamedly thrust herself into his hand, taking the hint, Blake plunged a finger deep into her. She whimpered into their kiss as her orgasm began to build. He removed his finger, sliding it up towards her clit. This time he inserted two fingers and continued to push in and out, hitting that magical spot each time. Before Serena knew it, she was tumbling over the edge, screaming into Blake's mouth as her orgasm unleashed.

Blake removed his fingers and managed to re-tie her bikini bottom. While Blake was attending to her clothing, Serena reached into his boardies and gripped his throbbing cock at the base before pumping up and down. Holding onto his neck with her other arm, she looked deftly into his eyes. They stared at one another as she continued to stroke his dick. A few strokes later, Blake was erupting into the ocean, grunting as Serena continued to stroke him.

When he finished, he leaned his forehead against hers, panting. "That was so much better than before." Serena pulled her head back and looked inquisitively at him. "Nothing, forget it," he murmured.

"Na, uhh, spill."

"I just did...into the ocean," Blake said with a cheeky grin, hoping to change the topic, but Serena wouldn't let it go. She stared at him until reluctantly he told her about what happened after seeing her get changed earlier.

"Hmmpf," was all she said, before crashing her lips to his once again. She wrapped her legs around his, holding him tightly with her arms and legs. She broke the kiss before she leaned to his ear and whispered, "I'm glad I was here for the second time." Biting on his earlobe gently, she then kissed along his jawline. All of a sudden, she pulled away and dove under the water, leaving a stunned Blake watching her perfect ass swim away from him.

In a short period of time, Blake was hooked and the happiest he had been in a long time.

CHAPTER 8

THE SUN HAD SET, AND IN ITS WAKE, LEFT BEHIND MILLIONS OF tiny stars flickering in the dark night sky; it was a very romantic setting. Blake and Serena walked back along the beach towards the resort, hand in hand, chatting and getting to know one another. Serena excitedly told him about starting her dream job when she got back. Blake mentioned that he was waiting to hear on a position change within his company, possibly with relocation. He'd be happy with either position but the living in limbo was starting to bug him. The way Serena and Blake had connected, you would think they have known each other for years, and not less than six hours.

When they returned to Oasis, they found Tom, Michele, Heather, and Robert all sitting at the beachfront bar. The girls were drinking decadent looking piña coladas out of coconuts and the boys a local beer our of massive beer steins.

"There they are," Michele said, her face beaming. Serena was unsure if it was due to the cocktails or from the handsome man sitting next to her. Heather and Robert looked up, smiled and then returned to their conversation. Heather had some serious flirty eyes going on and Robert seemed to be equally captivated.

"Hey," both Serena and Blake said in unison, before Serena sat next to Michele, giving her a shoulder bump and a wink. Blake stood behind Serena and wrapped his arms around her. She snuggled back into him and passed the beer that Tom handed her to Blake, while the bartender got to work on her cocktail.

Michele looked at Serena and smirked; Serena lifted her eyebrows and grinned back at her sister from another mister. Serena and Michele had been friends for three years, and even though no words were just spoken, their movements in themselves were a whole conversation.

The barman handed Serena her drink and her eyes bugged out of her head, she had never seen a more decadent looking cocktail in her life. She wrapped her lips around the straw and took a sip, moaning in pleasure as the creamy, liquid goodness snaked its way into her belly. She felt Blake's cock twinge at her back, so she took another sip and glanced over her shoulder, and stared directly at him. She moaned again, subtly rocking her hips into his cock as she did so. Blake gazed back at her, and without blinking, continued to rub himself along her lower back...*Two can play at this game,* she thought. Serena placed her drink onto the bar and lowered one arm; she bent it back and began to stroke Blake's cock through his boardies. Blake coughed and choked when he felt her hand on his cock; he wasn't expecting that.

"You right, babe?" Serena sassily asked as she glanced back over her shoulder at him. She winked and seductively smirked at him, before turning her attention back to her drink.

"Yeah, all good. Just went down the wrong hole," Blake replied as he leaned down. He gently sucked and nibbled on Serena's earlobe and whispered, "Game on, woman."

He snaked his hand around and squeezed her boob, as he ground his stiffening cock into her back. Serena melted into him and his touch, before she whispered back, "It's on like Donkey Kong." She turned her head to look up at him, both of their eyes ablaze with lust. She placed a chaste kiss on his cheek, before she stood up and headed towards Heather and Robert, swinging her ass from side to side as she sashayed away from him.

The six of them fell into easy conversation together and the evening was filled with fun and laughter. The air surrounding the bar was electric: sparks flying, the temperature rising, even though the sun had just set. As more drinks flowed, inhibitions were lowered; each of them sneaking kisses here and there, while hands were secretly, or not so secretly, groping and exploring.

Before they knew it, the beachfront bar was closing and darkness was well and truly upon them. While they leisurely walked away from the bar, back towards the resort main area, the conversation turned to dinner and continuing the party. After a debate as to whether it was pizza or Chinese, they finally agreed to meet in an hour at the resort pizza place.

CHAPTER 9

THE GIRLS GIGGLED AND LAUGHED ALL THE WAY BACK TO THE room, just like they did freshman year after an afternoon at McGee's. "We are so terrible," Michele stated. As they waited for the elevator, she punched the button calling for the lift.

"How so?" Heather asked, completely oblivious to what Michele was getting at.

"We, all three of us," pointing her fingers in circles at each of them, "didn't even last eight hours on our no boys rule."

"Have you seen the hotties that have attached to us?" Heather looked at Michele with raised eyebrows. Michele just stared back at her, not saying anything because

Heather was right. "I rest my case…besides there was no way in hell that rule was going to be enforced, right?"

Michele replied, "Yeah," while Serena just nodded her head in agreement.

The lift doors opened and the three girls climbed in and made their way up to their floor and room. Michele unlocked the door, stepping in; she held the door open for Heather and Serena. As Michele closed the door she declared, "Okay, twenty minutes to get ready and then we can have a quiet drink, just the three of us, before heading off for a night to remember."

"Sounds like a great plan to me." Serena walked towards her room, just as she went to close the door, Heather called out, "And, Serena, no more peep shows."

"Shut up, Heather," Serena snapped, flicking Heather the bird.

"Save the show for later," Michele said, as she pretended to grind herself on her doorway.

"You two are bitches. Go get dressed, Suzy Stripper here wants a quiet drink with her girls before we head out."

The three of them laughed as they each closed their doors to get ready.

Thirty minutes later, they were dressed to impress; Heather in a sexy as hell midnight blue halter dress, which hugged her curves and accentuated her tiny waist. Michele was wearing her ass-hugging jeans and aqua blue, one shoulder shirt that made her eyes bluer, if that was even possible, and Serena was wearing a mid-calf length, black and white, Aztec print strapless dress. Popping open a bottle of bubbly, they filled their glasses and headed out onto the balcony to enjoy a quiet drink together. The moonlight was sparkling on the pool water below, creating a magical view. Each of them gushed over the guys that they had met and were shocked that it took less than eight hours; that was a record for them.

Serena walked to the balcony edge and rested her elbows on the railing. Her eyes drifted down the beach and memories of earlier that afternoon came rushing back to her. Her neck and cheeks darkened as she remembered the feel of Blake's fingers inside her, the pressure of his hands as he caressed her body, and his mouth crashing against hers. Serena moaned, not so quietly, as she turned and sat down on the balcony lounge in the middle of the girls. Both Heather and Michele's eyes snapped towards her.

"Did you just remembergasm?" Heather enquired.

"What the hell is remembergasm?" Serena asked.

"Remembering an amazeballs off the charts orgasm that causes you to gasm again. Hence, remembergasm."

"Ummm…"

"We'll take that ummm as a yes," Michele said as she topped up each of their glasses. "Now, spill the deets, Serena. You've been glowing since you and Blake came back from your walk." She took a sip before adding, "And don't even say nothing happened, you totally have the gasm glow."

Serena stared at them both, wondering what to tell. She had never been one to share details like that before, probably because nothing like this had ever happened to her in her life. "I'm not one to flick an tell, sorry, girls."

"So he went to flick town, nice," Heather replied. "So, are we going to karaoke it up tonight?"

In unison, Michele and Serena both yell, "Hell no!" Followed by, "Jinx, Double jinx," and finally, "Jinx infinity."

Heather rolled her eyes at the jinx off, she never got the whole jinx game that Serena and Michele played.

After the laughter had subsided, Heather raised her almost empty glass. "A toast. To paradise, fucking hot men, and fantabolous orgasms."

They all giggled and hollered, "Cheers!" They clinked their glasses and drank, before they fell back into their usual chatter. When the bottle of bubbly was finished, Michele jumped up and shouted. "Okay, time to go meet the guys!"

The three girls, linked arms and made their way towards the lift to meet the guys for a night to remember.

CHAPTER 10

THE GUYS DASHED BACK TO THE ROOM, QUICKLY GRABBED showers and changed for the evening ahead. Thirty minutes later, they were on their way to the pizza place, each of them eager to meet up with the girls again. On the way to the restaurant, Robert aptly named Serena, Michele, and Heather, the sexy trio.

Once seated, they ordered a bucket of beers and garlic bread to nibble on while they waited. Blake waited for Robert to grill him about earlier; normally he'd have no qualms about sharing what happened with a chick, but this time, not so much. There was something different about Serena. He was drawn in a way like never before, and he was really hoping that it wouldn't just be a holiday fling. He really wanted it to lead to something permanent when they got back to the mainland. It was totally crazy to be thinking that, considering he'd only known her for less than eight hours. But to be honest, he knew more about her than any girl he had been with in the past; that in itself both scared and excited him.

The waitress had just delivered the breads when Tom spoke up, "So, this is a new way to spend our guys' getaway, but to be honest, this is the best one we have ever fuckin' been on."

"Fuck, yeah," Robert replied. "This is by far the best ever and it's only day one. No offense to you assholes, but I really want to spend more alone time with Heather and get to know her, and not just in my usual 'fuck em and chuck em' way."

Blake stared in shock, his beer frozen midway to his mouth. Tom, on the other hand, choked on his beer. When the coughing subsided, he stared at Robert and asked, "Dude, did you get too much sun today?"

Robert looked over his arms and asked, "No, why? Am I turning red?"

Tom shook his head again and chuckled as he said. "Never mind, Rob." Turning to Blake he mouthed, "What the fuck?"

Blake just shrugged his shoulders. "A toast." Raising his beer he proudly declared, "To Oasis."

"To Oasis," they all repeated, clinking their bottles before drinking and falling into their usual banter: Tom and Blake teasing Robert, and him not realising that they are taking the piss out of him.

The three of them continued to chat while waiting for the girls to arrive, each of them not so subtly glancing towards the door. They were eager for the girls to arrive and see where the night took them.

CHAPTER 11

THE SECOND BEER BUCKET HAD JUST ARRIVED WHEN THE HAIRS on the back of Blake's neck stood on end and his body tingled from head to toe. He spun around towards the bar entrance and in walked the girls. His eyes immediately landed on Serena and his eyes nearly popped out of his head; his cock twitched in agreement. She looked absolutely, fucking drop dead gorgeous in the black and white strapless dress. Blake noticed that every guy in the pizza joint was staring at the girls as they made there way over to the table. His inner caveman growled at them and the thought to himself; *She's mine, fuckers.*

Robert paused mid-sentence; his eyes followed Blake's towards the door. When he saw the girls, he immediately jumped up and raced over to Heather. Shocking Blake and

Tom, he wrapped his arms around her waist, dipped her back and kissed her senseless—it was very romantic and not Robert like at all. Once they had finished their dramatic PDA, he dragged her over to the table, and they sat very close together. Serena couldn't help but smile at how blissfully happy her friend was; she deserved all the happiness in the world and after a rough few months, she'd finally found her Ironman.

Tom walked over to Michele and placed a gentle kiss on her cheek. Serena noticed her friend's cheeks darken and a grin took over her face, while her blue eyes sparkled with desire. Tom laced his fingers with hers and escorted her back towards the table, pulling out her chair for her, ever the gentleman. In all the time Serena had known Michele, she had never seen her react to a guy like that before. She and Tom seemed perfect for each other; like they were fated to meet one another, their paths meant to cross.

Serena could not be happier for her both of her friends.

Blake was still sitting at the table, powerless to move. He sat there staring at Serena; she brushed a lock of hair behind her ear and smiled at him as she began to walk towards Blake. Her movements snapped him back to reality, and finally, he stood up. He gravitated towards her and when she was within arms reach, he reached out for her hand. The music and people around him faded away, the only person he could see was Serena. She gripped his hand and quietly whispered, "Hi." That one word sent shockwaves through his body.

"You looking fucking stunning, Serena," he said, as he leaned forward and placed a slow and sensual kiss on her lips. Pulling back, he looked deep into her eyes. "Shall we?" he asked. Serena nodded, unable to speak; she was completely nervous all of a sudden. He placed his hand on her lower back, causing her skin to prickle as he ushered her towards the table. Stopping, he pulled her chair out for her and winked as she sat down; with that wink, her insides danced with desire. If she weren't already sitting down, she would have fallen into a heap. His smile made her weak at the knees and left her feeling giddy with need and desire; her panties damp with arousal.

By time Serena and Blake had joined them, and had taken their seats, the waitress was leaving the table, drinks and dinner order in hand. The girls decided to stick with bubbly and ordered a bottle...after all; it was cheaper that way. They also ordered another beer bucket for the guys and three pizzas to share.

Just like earlier at the beach bar, the six of them fell into easy conversation as a group and each couple continued to click perfectly together. To anyone watching, you'd think they were three couples away together and not two separate groups who had only met eight hours earlier. After dinner, they decided to head to Hanttula's, the resort's tiki bar for a night of dancing...and more drinks.

After a few drinks, Heather and Robert headed for the dance floor and began to grind and dirty dance with each one another, oblivious to everyone else in the room; their friends included. Serena noticed that they were totally lost in one another, and she couldn't help but smile and be happy for her friend. Tom and Michele headed to the bar for another round of drinks, while Blake and Serena stayed at the table. By then, they were sitting dangerously close to one another, the heat radiating off them was scorching hot. They gazed at one another and were completely lost in each other's eyes but were snapped back to reality when Heather and Robert rejoined them; they were laughing their asses off at something from earlier in the day. Soon after, Tom and Michele returned with the drinks: a tray of tequila shots, three beers, and three bubblies—the tiki bar didn't serve by the bottle...responsible drinking and all that shit. They each grabbed a shot, raised the glasses in a toast, and shouted "Cheers!" before throwing them back, slamming the empty glasses on the table.

Serena coughed and spluttered, scrunching her face up. "Ugh, that's fuckin' nasty."

Michele whacked Tom in the stomach and scoffed, "Told you she'd say that and pull that face." She smirked and looked smug as she said this.

"Up yours, bitch," Serena replied before blowing her a kiss. She grabbed her bubbly and took a big sip to erase the horrible tequila taste from her mouth.

Blake rubbed Serena's back. "You okay, sweetness?"

Serena melted at the endearing term Blake just used. "Yeah, I'm all good. Just really don't like tequila. I'm more of a Sour Puss girl."

Blake jumped up and kissed Serena on the cheek. "Back in a sec."

Before he had taken two steps, the DJ announced. "... and up next, we have Blake singing 'My Girl'." He paused midstep, turned towards Robert, shot daggers at him with his eyes, pointed, and shouted. "You're a fucker!"

Robert shrugged his shoulders and hollered, "WOOHOO, go, Blake!"

Blake, not one to turn down a dare; especially one from Robert, turned towards the stage, gave him the middle finger over his shoulder, and jumped up next to the DJ. Grabbing the microphone, he prepared to sing. Getting right into it, he belted out a not half-bad rendition of 'My Girl.' The whole crowd erupted into applause when he'd finished. Taking a bow, he handed the mic back to the DJ, hopped off the stage, and strutted back over to the group. He sucker punched Robert in the arm, called him an asshole, again, and stormed away from them. Everyone, except Robert, was laughing. Serena stopped laughing and sadly watched Blake storm off. She looked towards Tom and asked, "Should I go and see if he's okay?"

Tom looked over at her and shook his head. "Yeah. Nah, leave him be. These two do this sort of shit all the time." Taking a sip of beer, he looked towards Robert and with a smirk added, "Blake will get his revenge, just you wait."

"Fuckin', bring it," Robert replied, before he turned his attention back towards Heather; he was totally smitten with the brown-haired beauty, and she was also.

Five minutes later, Blake returned to the table with another tray of shots, his anger from before gone, replaced with fun and a jovial smile. He placed four shots of red stuff in front of Serena and with a grin proudly stated, "Sour Puss, just for you." He pulled her into his side and tucked her under his arm, before he kissed her on the temple.

Serena sat there, staring at the shots and smiling. No guy had ever been this nice, or thoughtful, towards her before. She glanced up at Blake and whispered, "Thanks." She wrapped her arm around his waist and rubbed his side. "Are you okay? You seem pissed off over the 'My Girl' thing."

"Nah, yeah, it's all good, babe." A little louder he added, "I'll get my revenge…" He paused for effect before adding, whilst he stared directly at Robert, "I'll get him back when he least expects it."

"Pfft, whatevs, asshole," Robert replied, a flicker of fear

flashed on his face as he picked up his beer, staring intently at Blake.

Blake passed out the rest of the shots; his eyes checked to make sure everyone had a shot and his gaze landed on Robert's. He chuckled to himself as Robert raised his shot glass and shouted, "Bottoms up, bitches!" Lifting the shot glass to his lips, Blake's eyes were locked on Robert. Just as Robert took the shot, he began to laugh. Robert spat the liquid back out of his mouth, across the table. "Ugh, what the fuck?"

"Told you I'd get ya." He looked towards everyone and proudly declared, "Vinegar with lime juice."

Everyone burst out laughing, everyone except for Robert that was. He grumbled, "Shut up, fuckers."

Robert pouted, before he reached over and snatched the shot from Blake's hands. He lifted it to his nose, sniffed, and when it passed the sniff test, he threw it back. Slamming the glass down, he stood up, grabbed Heather's hand, and they headed towards the dance floor. Tom was still laughing, holding his stomach with tears in his eyes. "Dude, that was gold! You got him good, but you do realise that he's going to retaliate, right?"

Shrugging his shoulders, Blake replied, "Bring it." He then grabbed another tequila shot and handed Serena a Sour Puss shot. He looked directly into her eyes for he said, "Cheers, to an amazing getaway."

Serena pursed her lips and quietly murmured in reply, "Cheers to that."

They saluted each other before chugging back two shots in a row. Serena and Blake stared at one another, not saying a word, the air around them oozing with lust. Serena licked her bottom lip before gently biting it, swallowing deeply. She was just about to ask Blake if he

wanted to get out of there when the DJ announced. "…
annnnd up next, we have the troublesome trio with
'Wannabe'."

Serena snapped back to reality when she heard their
unofficial college nickname and whispered, "Ohh no she
didn't". She looked across the table to see Michele in a fit
of laughter. From the dance floor, they heard Heather zeal-
ously shout. "Let's go, bitches!"

Heather grabbed Michele, who grabbed Serena, and
the three of them headed towards the stage and DJ. They
jumped up on the platform and grabbed a mic each. As
soon as the opening laugh blasted through the speakers,
they jumped into action, laughing and singing. Without
missing a beat, Michele, Heather, and Serena danced and
sang "Wannabe" with flair and pizazz, as if they were
members of the group. The crowd erupted into applause
when they were finished. They each took a bow and
stepped off the stage. In a fit of giggles, they headed back
to the table, where the three guys were still cheering for
them.

"That was fucking awesome," Tom declared, as he
wrapped his arms around Michele, pulling her into to him.
She snuggled into his embrace before he spun her around,
kissing her deeply. Breaking the kiss, he grabbed her hand,
and led her towards the dance floor.

Serena and Blake stared at one another before he put
his hand out. "May I have this dance?" he asked, his tone
low and gravelly, causing Serena to melt from the
inside out.

"Why certainly, sir," Serena answered. She stood up
and curtseyed like that did back in the day. They linked
hands and laughed on their way to the dance floor. They
pushed through the crowd until they were in the center;

Blake wrapped his arms around Serena's waist and pulled her in close. Serena draped her arms around his neck, closed her eyes, and rested her head on his shoulder. Their hips swayed to the beat of the music until the song changed and the tempo increased. Serena opened her eyes and noticed her friends were in similar positions. Each of them dancing perilously close to their partner, the heat radiating from them was off the charts.

Heather and Robert hadn't been seen since the girls sang, but one could guess what they were up to. After a few more drinks, the remaining two couples each broke away and their first night is paradise went off with a bang…between the sheets.

Serena and Blake left Tom and Michele on the dance floor and headed towards the beach. When they passed the cabanas, Blake made a detour towards the one at the far end. He sat down and pulled Serena between his legs, he wrapped his arms around her thighs and rested his head on her stomach. He squeezed her ass and gripped her tighter. Serena ran her fingers through his hair when he began to place gentle kisses along her clothed belly. She closed her eyes and lost herself in the moment, moaning and gently pushing herself closer to Blake. Bunching her dress at her hips, he kissed along her abdomen, his lips left her skin prickling and on fire. Serena groaned when his lips touched her skin. She threw her head back as the electricity spread through her body; this was singularly the most erotic moment of her life. He slid his hands down her thighs, before inching his fingers under the back of her dress and cupping her ass; he squeezed her cheeks as he tugged her closer to him. He pushed her dress up at the front again and kissed her throbbing mound over her panties. "Blake," Serena whimpered into the night sky, as he slipped a finger inside her panties and skimmed it up and down her slit.

"You're so wet," he murmured, as he sank his finger deep inside her wet channel. At the intrusion, Serena's legs buckled under her, and she fell onto Blake, pushing him back onto the cabana lounge. Straddling him, he continued to plunge his finger in and out; his movements were limited due to her panties. With his other hand, he tore them off, throwing the tattered material to the ground. With room to move, he thrust two fingers into her, flicking her G-spot, while simultaneously rubbing her clit with his thumb. The pressure on her clit set her whole body on fire, and she exploded around his fingers, screaming his name into the night sky.

When Blake withdrew his fingers, he licked her juices off them as he stared intently up at her straddling him. Serena's eyes were sparkling in the moonlight. He sat up and wrapped his arms around her shoulders, his lips crashed against hers as they kissed. She rocked her hips on his cock before she pulled back. With shaking fingers, she unbuckled his pants and freed his cock. Once it sprang free, she leaned forward and licked the bead of precum from the tip, before sucking it deep into her mouth. Blake moaned as he reached down to grab a condom from his pants pocket, tearing it open with his teeth.

"No," Serena panted. Blake paused, and looked at her intently. "Let me," she whispered. She took the condom from him, and with trembling hands, sheathed his cock. Pushing up on her knees, she teased the tip of his cock at her entrance before she sank herself on him; both of them moaning at the feeling of her sliding down his shaft. Once she had taken him to the hilt, she circled her hips before she began to ride him.

Blake sat up as he wrapped his arms around her lower back and pulled her forward. He pulled the top of her dress down and shoved his face into her tits. She continued to slide up and down his cock. She threw her arms around his neck and held Blake closer to her, their bodies slick with sweat as they continued to move in sync. He slid his hand between them and began to rub her clit in circles, while he continued to nuzzle her breasts. "I'm coming," Serena whisper-shouted, as her orgasm rocked through her body. With a grunt, Blake soon followed, stilling as he erupted inside of her.

They stay enfolded in each other arms, resting their heads together until their breathing returned to normal. She climbed off and lay back, while Blake removed the condom. He dropped it onto the sand before he lay back down next to her. Wrapped in each other's embrace, they stayed in each other's arms and stared up at the night sky. There they fell asleep on the cabana, half-dressed, content and longing for a future together.

CHAPTER 12

THE NEXT MORNING, THEY ALL MET FOR BREAKFAST AT Frenchie's, the resort's 60's style diner. It had black and white checkered floors and red vinyl booths along the sidewalls. The kitchen was at the back, with a huge narrow serving window, so you could see in. There was a counter in front with black steel stools and at one end were an old school cash register and an old-fashioned juke box. Sporadically in the middle there were square tables with black chairs; it was very retro but in a modern way.

Heather and Robert were the last to arrive and were extremely hungover and not very talkative. They ordered coffees to go and left as soon as they were delivered. They headed back to Robert's room to sleep off their hangovers, telling the group they'd meet for lunch later today.

The waitress returned with the coffees and took their breakfast order. Serena wrapped her fingers around the mug and took a sip of the heavenly brew. She closed her eyes and moaned, causing memories of last night to come rushing back. She clenched her thighs together to squash the tingly feeling building deep in her nether regions; the pressure caused another groan to slip through her lips. She opened her eyes to be met with the three of them staring at her. Tom looked stunned, Blake was heatedly staring back, and Michele grinned at her friend and mouthed, "Remembergasm?" Serena nodded and took another sip of coffee. As she swallowed, she wondered how she was going to get out of this awkward moment but the attention was taken off Serena as the server arrived with their breakfast...she had never been so thankful for a waitress interruption.

After breakfast, Serena, Michele, Blake, and Tom decided to explore the island together. They rented bikes and went for a ride before they walked along the beach, chatting and getting to know one another. The four of them clicked on so many levels. Serena linked her fingers with Blake's, and he pulled her in close, and kissed her temple. Wrapping her arm around him, she held him tight. A wave of sadness appeared out of nowhere when she realised that in six days time they would be going back to their lives...separately. The sadness increased, causing her to shiver, Blake felt her shudder in his arms, "What you thinking, pretty lady?"

"Nothing," Serena quietly replied and looked down at her feet, absentmindedly drawing circles in the sand with her toes.

Blake stopped and with his finger under her chin, lifted Serena's head so she was looking directly at him. "I don't buy that for a second, wanna try again, sweetness?"

Every time Blake used an endearing term with her, her insides melted and she fell deeper in lust with him. "It's nothing, really, I'm...I'm just being silly." She pulled away from him and walked towards the palms lining the white sand and took a seat leaning against the trunk.

"Serena, I may have only known you for less than twenty-four hours, but I can tell that something is bothering you. Talk to me." She looked up at him and sighed as her eyes welled with tears, thankful that her sunnies were covering her eyes. He sat down next to Serena and stared at her. "Talk to me."

Serena dug her toes into the sand; literally and figuratively, taking a deep breath she replied. "It's just...I... umm, was just thinking about not seeing you when we get back to the mainland and it made me sad."

"We still could, Serena." He looked intently at her as he said this, half-questioning and half-stating.

She sadly shook her head sideways, "How? We don't even live near each other. You're still waiting on a possible job position and location change to who-knows-where, and no offence, but the long distance thing isn't for me. Blake, this is just going to have be a wonderful holiday fling and that makes me happy, but I'm also sad that in six days it will all end."

"Well, looks like we have a lot to pack into six days then." Blake stood up, turned around and pulled Serena up before he threw her over his shoulder. He ran for the ocean and she playfully squealed and laughed.

"No, no, no!" Serena shouted, but her efforts were futile, because Blake raced into the sea, and threw her through the air into the cold water. Serena came up coughing and spluttering. Blake stood there grinning at her. "You are dead, mister!" she shouted, as she pushed her hair out of her eyes.

"Bring it," Blake retorted, as he jumped towards her, taking her down in a spectacular tackle. While they were under the water, Blake wrapped his arms tightly around her, his lips found hers, and as they floated towards the surface, he kissed her. When their heads were finally above the water, Serena wrapped her legs around him and they continued to kiss, completely enthralled with one another.

The squealing of Michele broke the moment; they looked towards the beach, to see Tom chasing her up the shoreline. He reached out, grabbed her around the waist and turned around; he headed straight into the water, dunking them both.

When they both surfaced, Michele was snort laughing and what passed between Tom and her was electric; blind Freddie could see the connection between the two of them. She jumped into his arms, their lips crashed together, the force knocked Tom back, but he held tight to Michele. Their kiss heated up and was only broken when Blake splashed them and cleared his throat in a 'get a room' kind of way. With his arm still wrapped tightly around Michele, Tom splashed back but he completely missed them. Serena and Blake laughed and together they splashed and saturated Michele and Tom.

Michele pulled away from Tom, "Ohh, it's on now." She proceeded to splash them back, actually hitting them this time. The four of them laughed as an epic water fight started. It ended up being girls versus boys until it was each man, or woman, for himself or herself. The splashing subsided and when no winner was declared, they decided to head back to the resort for a change of clothes, followed by lunch, and then an afternoon of poolside chilaxing, cocktails, and fun.

Once back at the resort, they split up to get changed and agreed to meet back at the pool bar in thirty minutes…maybe longer because each of them stopped off at separate bars for a sneaky drink; the boys at the bar from last night and the girls at the pool bar.

CHAPTER 13

TOM UNLOCKED THE DOOR AND WALKED INTO THE ROOM first, he abruptly stopped, causing Blake to bump into him. They fell into the room further to be met with Robert's bare ass. He had Heather bent over the back of the couch. The door slamming shut, and the shuffle, garnered the attention of Robert and Heather. Heather squealed in embarrassment as she quickly shoved Robert off of her and pulled her dress down. Her face was beetroot red but Robert was unfazed. "Hey guys," he said without a care in the world. He pulled Heather into his side and tucked her under his arm; she squirmed and refused to look over at Tom and Blake.

"Hey," Blake and Tom casually replied.

"Umm, Heather, the girls are in your room getting ready for lunch," Tom said, not looking directly at her.

"Yeah, thanks," she quickly replied before she speedily headed straight for the door.

Robert pulled her back to him and deeply kissed her goodbye, he was completely oblivious to her embarrassment. "See you soon, babe," he said, swatting her ass as she walked away.

Heather screeched in shock at the ass tap. "Yep, I'll, ahh, catch ya's later," Heather mumbled, looking down at her feet, and not at Tom or Blake, as she hastily exited the room, completely mortified. She slammed the door behind her and made a beeline for the lifts.

At the sound of the door slamming, the guys awkwardly stared at one another, no one uttering a word. A few moments later, Tom walked over to the minibar and grabbed out three beers, handing each guy one.

"Thanks," Robert said, as he took the beer that Tom offered him. "So, how was the beach?" Robert was not at all fazed or embarrassed about what the guys just walked in on.

"It was good," Blake replied after taking a sip of beer. "I'm guessing you're feeling better now?"

Robert looked at them over his beer. "I'm a gentleman and will not fuck and tell, BUT I will say, I'm feeling relieved...if you get my drift."

Blake shook his head, after all these years, Robert still managed to shock him with his actions. "Yeah, we get it." Taking another drink, he then asked, "You coming to lunch with us?"

"Sounds great. I also booked us on that jet ski tour tomorrow morning."

"Wow, you have been a busy boy this morning," Tom mocked, as he picked up Robert's shirt and threw it at him, before ducking into his room to shower and change for lunch.

Blake laughed and headed to his room to get ready to meet the girls.

"Guess I'll just wait here then," Robert announced to the then empty room. He grabbed another beer and sat back on the lounge to wait. Putting his feet up on the coffee table, he noticed Heather's discarded panties. He bent down, picked them up, and tucked them into his pocket to return to her at lunch...or to keep—anything was possible with Robert.

CHAPTER 14

HEATHER HAD NEVER BEEN SO MORTIFIED OR EMBARRASSED IN her entire life, and she had done some stupid shit. She raced out of the room quicker than a fat dude could inhale a bucket of chicken from *KFC*. She unlocked the room door and raced inside, making a beeline for the minibar; she cracked open a beer and chugged it.

"Rough morning?" Serena enquired, of her clearly distressed friend.

Heather was so in her own head, she hadn't even noticed Serena sitting there and jumped in fright. She grabbed another beer and plonked herself down on the couch next to Serena. She placed her beer down on the coffee table and laid her head in Serena's lap, staring up at her friend, she said, "I have never been so embarrassed in my life." Heather sighed loudly and then added, "Never. Ever. Before." Pausing between each word for emphasis.

"What happened?" Michele asked as she walked into the lounge room, towel-drying her hair.

Serena began to run her fingers through Heather's hair, trying to relax her.

In a rushed breath, she told them, "Robert and I got caught."

"Caught doing what?" Michele asked, as she sat on the coffee table with a worried look on her face. She immediately began to think the worst.

"Mid-coitus," Heather quietly told them.

Serena and Michele both burst out laughing. Heather sat up, crossed her legs, reached for her beer, and chugged the rest of it before cracking open the other and taking a big gulp. "It's not funny, you bitches."

"It totally is," Serena said in between snorts, tears were pouring down her face. "How? What happened?"

"After breakfast, Robert and I went back to his room. We climbed into bed and fell asleep. We woke up, and had a sexy time shower together." She lifted her eyebrows in a suggestive way. "Then we were in the lounge chatting. I was leaving to come back here, get changed for lunch, and wait for you guys. We were walking towards the door and he kissed me goodbye. It umm, ahh got heated, really heated and one thing led to another. He backed us towards the lounge; in a flash my dress was around my ears and my panties were gone. He bent me over the back of the couch, and well...you know. Then the guys walked in; the door slamming shut signaling their arrival. I quickly pulled my dress down and got out of there. I've never been so embarrassed in my life." She took another gulp of beer. "Hence, the beer chugging."

Serena and Michele burst out laughing...again. "You two are such bitches," Heather whined.

Michele leant forward and rubbed her knee. "Hey, if it was one of us, you would totally be laughing your ass off, too. Embarrassment aside, at least you're getting some. Apart from some awesome make out sessions and heavy petting, no sex for me." She got up and grabbed three beers from the minibar; which was more a real bar because it was fully stocked and not so mini. She returned to the couch and handed them to the girls before she sat back on the coffee table.

"Really?" Heather and Serena asked shocked and in unison.

"Jinx," Serena said. Heather rolled her eyes, shaking her head.

"Really, really," Michele said in a Donkey from *Shrek* way. "But, I'm happy, deliriously happy. Tom is an amazing man. We have actually talked about keeping in touch when we get back."

"Robert and I don't do much talking, so I don't know what will happen with us but I hope to see him again when we get back." Opening her beer, she then asked, "How about you, S?" Looking towards Serena as she took another sip of beer.

"It will just be an Oasis fling for us. I'm not into the long-distance thing, besides he's waiting on a job change, and I'm starting my career when we get back." She shook her head and added, "I don't want the added pressure of long-distance." Serena stood up and headed into her room to finish getting ready for lunch, but all she could think about was, what if her and Blake did give it a go?

Could they have a future when they returned to the mainland?

Could she do the long-distance thing?

No, she decided that with Blake and her: what happens in Oasis would stay at Oasis.

CHAPTER 15

THE NEXT FOUR DAYS WERE SPENT THE SAME WAY, THE SIX OF them hanging out together. There were only two occasions when they weren't. Once, when the guys played a round of golf and the girls went to the spa. The second time was when the guys did their jet-ski tour. The girls lazed by the pool and soaked up the sun's rays while they were off jet-skiing.

After dinner last night, things got interesting to say the least.

For something different, they took a trip to the resort next door, Beaches, for an eighties' night. They had been dancing for a while when Serena needed to pee. She excused herself and headed towards the bathrooms. You could not wipe the smile off her face; the last few days had been amazing and she was ecstatically happy. She was a few paces from the bathroom door, when a noise down the hall around the corner caught her attention. Cautiously she headed towards the sound, she was shocked by what she saw. A redheaded girl was pinned to the wall by a guy; one of his hands covered her mouth and the other was fiddling with his fly. The girl began to whimper loudly at the sounds of his zipper lowering. Growling at her he yelled, "Shut it, bitch!" By that point, her dress was bunched around her waist, exposing her pink panties; she began thrashing about but he was too strong for her.

Without thinking, Serena stalked towards the asshole and girl. "Stop, get off her!" she shouted, as she grabbed his arm. He spun around on his heel, his eyes locked on Serena; they were full of rage and his pupils appeared dilated. He was obviously on something. Adrenalin took over her body and she launched herself at him. The asshole let go of the girl and then directed his attention to Serena. With the palm of his hand, he forcefully pushed Serena in the chest, shoving her with a thwack into the wall. She dropped to the floor with a thump on her ass. The chick quickly took off, and left Serena alone with him in the dimly lit hallway.

She tried to get up, but he violently pushed her back down and straddled her thighs, he had her trapped. Her heart began beating erratically; her breaths came in short, sharp bursts. She opened her mouth to scream but nothing came out, she was frozen with terror. Fear was coursing through her veins and her vision started to blur. He reared his arm back to hit her, when all of sudden, he was wrenched off her and thrown against the wall. Robert punched the asshole in the face twice before he shoved him into the corner. He spun around and crouched down to see if Serena was okay. Through tears, Serena nodded her head and Robert carefully wrapped his arms around her.

All of a sudden, the hallway was filled with people, the chatter extremely loud and overwhelming for Serena. Robert sensed her tense and he helped her to stand up. As she stood up, she became overwhelmed, her vision started to fade, and she collapsed into his arms. She vaguely heard Blake's voice as the darkness took over.

When she came to, she was lying on the couch in their room. Her head was in Heather's lap and she was gently rubbing a wet cloth across her forehead, soothingly stroking her arm. "Hey, welcome back to the land of the living," Heather said with a smile.

"What happened?" She looked around and realised she was back at Oasis and in the safety of her room. She had no recollection of leaving the bar next door. "How did I get back here?" she softly asked.

Heather was in full nurse mode at that moment. She lifted Serena's head off her lap and crouched by the couch, squeezing Serena's hand. "What do you remember, sweet pea?"

Serena shuffled so she was then sitting up. "I remember walking to the bathroom. Seeing a guy hurting someone. Pushing him and then it's all jumbled." She paused and gasped in shock, as the events from earlier came crashing back to her, her eyes welled with tears. Heather hopped back up onto the couch and pulled Serena into her arms. Hugging her tightly, she let Serena cry it all out. She rubbed her back in circles and whispered, "SHHHH, let it all out," over and over again as her friend fell apart in her arms.

Serena noticed Michele walk over to them with a glass

of water. Michele placed the water on the coffee table and joined in on the hug when she saw how broken her friend was. "Thank God you are okay," she whispered. "I was so bloody worried about you."

The three of them sat there, hugging until they were interrupted by a knock on the door. Michele pulled away to answer it. She opened the door and Blake, Tom, and Robert were standing there, worry etched on each of their faces. Over Michele's shoulder, Blake saw Serena in Heather's arms crying and he raced into the room.

Serena looked up and when she saw him, she jumped up into his arms and broke down in tears, all over again. Blake wrapped his arms tightly around Serena. "Shhhh, it's okay. I've got you," he whispered while he gently rubbed her back. She closed her eyes and relaxed into him, Blake gave her all the comfort that she needed; this fact surprised Serena, considering she had only known Blake for a few days.

Eventually, Serena opened her eyes again; she saw Michele wrapped in Tom's arms, and Robert and Heather were deep in conversation by the balcony doors. Robert looked over at Serena and smiled, she pulled away from Blake and paced over to Robert. "Thank you," she murmured, as she wrapped her arms around him and burst into tears once again.

Robert was a little awkward to begin with, but he eventually placed his arms around her and hugged her back. Serena pulled away and looked up at him and said, "You saved, me, Robert." Swallowing back a sob she then said, "Thank you."

"It was nothing, Serena. Anyone would have done it," he replied, not wanting the attention or praise.

Shaking her head, she wiped away her tears. "No, not everyone would have done that. I appreciate it."

"Yeah, dude, Serena's right," Blake interjects. "You saved her tonight. You're a hero."

Robert was uncomfortable receiving all the praise, he was just glad that Serena was unhurt. "I'm glad you're okay. I'm, ahh, gonna head back to our room. I'm beat."

"I'll come with you," Heather said, she turned to Serena and asked. "Will you be okay if I go?"

Serena nodded her head, while at the same time both Serena and Blake spoke.

"Yeah, I'm okay." Serena said.

While Blake said, "I'll stay with her."

Heather looked to Blake. "Thanks, Blake. Please keep an eye on my girl here." She hugged him before she turned to Serena. "Rest up, lady, call me if you need anything."

"Yes, Mum," Serena said dryly, and started to feel like herself again with that comment.

"Yep, you'll be fine." Heather smirked as she kissed Serena on the cheek and followed Robert out of the room.

While they were all chatting, Tom and Michele ducked into her room and they could hear laughter and a movie playing.

Blake looked to Serena. "What do you want to do, sweetness?"

"I'm really tired, I'm just going to head to bed." Blake looked sad, thinking she that wanted to go to bed alone. "Will you hold me, please, Blake?"

In two steps, Blake had his arms wrapped around her. She started to cry again, so he picked her up in his arms and stalked into her room, gently closing the door behind him. He carefully laid her down on the bed before he kicked off his shoes and climbed in next to her. She snuggled into his side and gripped his shirt tightly in her fist as she continued to cry. He rubbed her arm soothingly and held her tight as she fell apart. "I was so scared, Blake," she blubbered.

"So was I," he replied, as he placed a kiss her on the temple.

"I had to step in, I couldn't leave her," she said on a sob.

"I know you couldn't, that's just the person you are. I'm proud that you stepped in, Serena. Not many people would have." He pulled her closer to him and held her tightly. "You're selflessness is one of the many things that I lo...like about you, Serena." She draped her arm across his stomach and snuggled into him, her head on his chest, the even beats of his heart calmed her.

Eventually they both fell asleep wrapped in each other's arms.

CHAPTER 16

THE NEXT MORNING WAS QUIET AND SUBDUED, THE EVENTS from last night were still fresh in everyone's mind. They all decided that a day lazing by the pool and chilaxing was just what the doctor ordered...and Robert deemed himself said doctor. Even after the decision was made, the mood was still very somber, compared to the previous days, but a quiet day was exactly what everyone needed to recharge and hopefully forget.

Each of them lazed in the sun, or swam in the pool, and processed what had happened yesterday; it was the perfect way to revitalise. By midmorning, Serena seemed to perk up and her change seemed to spark the group and the fun times, surely but slowly returned.

It was midafternoon, the sun was high in the sky and

the atmosphere had returned to almost normal. The guys had just ordered another round of beers and Michele and Heather ordered a third...or maybe forth bottle of wine. Their drinks were delivered and Heather played waitress. She handed the boys their beers and poured the wine. She offered one to Serena but she declined. "I've got water, I'm fine thanks."

Heather looked at her stunned, she had never, ever in the entire time they had known one another, turned down a wine. "Are you sure?"

"Yep, I'm sure, besides water is like wine," she stated.

"How so?" Heather asked, not quite sure what Serena was getting at.

"Well, Jesus turned water into wine, so it's kinda like the same thing, just different."

They all laughed at Serena's comparison and then fell back into their easy conversation, just like they previously had. The rest of the day was spent as Dr. Robert prescribed: lounging by the pool, chillaxing, swimming, and drinking copious amounts of alcohol.

That evening, after dinner, rather than head off together as a group to the bar like the previous nights, they all broke off into pairs. Heather and Robert headed to the bar for a game of pool, more drinks, and dancing. Tom and Michele decided to head back to the room for a quiet night in with a bottle of wine and watching *Thor*. Michele had a major thing for Loki and Tom kind of looked like him, so it was no wonder Michele was smitten. Serena asked Blake if they could go to their spot on the beach and he was happy to oblige. They grabbed a blanket, and a bottle of wine, and headed towards the beach and their spot for a quiet night, just the two of them.

Blake spread the blanket out and rested against a palm

tree. Serena sat in between Blake's legs, her back to his front, and leaned into him, making herself at home. He wrapped his arms around her and kissed her ear; she melted into his chest when she felt his lips on her. They quietly stared at the night sky, the only sound was the lapping of the water are the shore's edge and the beating of their hearts...creating the perfect moment.

Serena turned her head to look up at Blake. "Thank you," she whispered.

He bent his head down and kissed the tip of her nose. "You're welcome, but what are you thanking me for?"

"This past week has been amazing and I think it's because of you," she happily stated, staring into his eyes. "You gave me the strength to go on after the other night, I can never repay you for that."

"I agree, this week has been amazing. I'm glad I was there for you," pausing he swallowed deeply, "...and I really wish you'd reconsider about meeting up when we get back."

"Blake, please don't ruin this moment. I know I'm being a selfish bitch, but I just can't." She spun around to face him and placed a gentle but heartfelt kiss on his lips. She rested her forehead on his. "Let's pop open that bottle of wine and enjoy what time we have left at Oasis." Serena cupped his cheeks in her hands and lowered her lips to his. Increasing the pressure, she slipped her tongue into his mouth, plunging it in and out. She hoped this kiss would convey to Blake how she felt about him and the sorrow about her feelings when they returned home. Breaking the kiss, Blake sighed and sadly smiled up at Serena. Pulling back, he lifted her chin with his finger and looked deep into her eyes. "Serena, I will do anything for you, and I hope with everything that our paths do cross again one day." He lowered his head and placed his lips against hers again, increasing the pressure; his tongue darted out, seeking entry. Serena closed her eyes and opened her mouth, giving him access, their tongues caressed as they become one. She lifted up and straddled his hips; she wrapped her arms tightly around his neck as their kiss deepened. They lost themselves in each other and kissed like their lives depended on it. Blake broke the kiss, pulling away to rest his forehead against hers. "Serena, I...I think we should open that bottle of wine before this goes any further. My will around you is weak, and right at this moment, I would love nothing more than to make love to you right here under the stars."

Breathlessly she replied, "Yep, umm, yeah, okay." Serena climbed off his lap and sat next to him. She grabbed the glasses, while he cracked open the wine and poured them each each a drink. After a toast, Serena looked into Blake's eyes and murmured, "For the record, I wouldn't have minded your previous suggestion." She winked at him, before she settled back in between his legs, snuggling into him.

For the rest of the night, they talked about anything and everything, laughing and enjoying each other's company. After they finished the wine, they lay next to one another and stared at the night sky, both of them thinking about what-ifs and the future. Blake hoped that in the next two days that he could convince Serena to change her mind and give it a go when they got back. And Serena wished that she wasn't so scared to give Blake a chance at a future with her when they returned.

In the early hours of the morning, they fell asleep wrapped in each other's arms, happy yet sad at the same time.

CHAPTER 17

IT WAS THE LAST DAY AT OASIS AND TOMORROW THEY WOULD each return to the real world and adulthood. The atmosphere at breakfast was quiet and subdued, not like it normally was; everyone was deep in his or her own thoughts...and hungover.

After breakfast they headed to the beach for a game of sand volleyball. After the girls kicked the boys' asses, twice, they headed back to the pool and spent the rest of the day hanging out there, drinking cocktails, and enjoying their last moments at Oasis.

To do something different on the last night, they decided to go straight to Hanttula's for one last hurrah before returning to the reality tomorrow. Upon arrival, they discovered it was two-for-one drinks, dollar cheeseburgers, and karaoke night…again. Heather and Robert jumped with excitement and just like every time they had been there, they signed up for karaoke. Blake and Serena snagged what had unofficially become 'their' table near the windows overlooking the beach, while Michele and Tom headed to the bar to get the first round of drinks.

Before long, Heather and Robert were up on stage singing, "You're The One That I Want," from *Grease*. Surprisingly, they sounded amazeballs up there; they were much better then the first night singing together. The crowd went wild for them; cheering and hollering when the song finished. They hopped off the stage and made their way over to the rest of the group. Robert stopped and talked to the DJ, both of them were laughing as he turned around. His eyes landed on Blake and he smirked at him, before he raced over to catch up to Heather, who was heading towards the bar.

Heather and Robert returned with a tray of shots and six cocktails; Heather put her foot down and there was to be no beer or wine consumed that night. Her exact words were, "It's our last night, and we go hard." It really wasn't hard to convince any of them, one last hurrah was definitely called for.

They each downed a shot before Robert piped up, surprising everyone with his words, "To new friends and new relationships. And a great fucking week at Oasis." Everyone raised their second shots in toast before slamming them back. Robert coughed and spluttered, "Fuck you, Blake, again?"

"What?" Blake asked, not sure what Robert was getting at, but Heather burst out laughing.

"Surprise," she said, winking at Robert, while she laughed her ass off.

"You did that?" he asked, his voice laced with admiration, a touch of anger, and a smidge of amazement. She nodded her head and winked at him, as she sipped on her cocktail. "I'm impressed but this means war, baby."

"Bring it," she countered, as she placed her hands on her hips, challenging him. He jumped up and headed towards her but he stopped midstep as the DJ said, "And up next is Blake."

Robert turned to Blake and grinned. "You're up, asshole."

"You're a fucker!" Blake shouted across the table and shook his head; not at all surprised that Robert would do this on the last night. He just sat there but didn't move.

"Go on, you can do it," Serena said, as she nudged him in the ribs and winked. Blake remained seated, the previous nights he had pretended to be pissed off but tonight he wasn't pretending. Robert had done this every night and tonight Blake just wanted to relax and have fun.

"Come on up, Blake," the DJ announced again.

"Nope, not happening," Blake declared, as he folded his arms across his chest.

Serena jumped up and said, "Fine, I'll do it." She downed the rest of her drink, before she kissed Blake deeply, and then she skipped over to the DJ. She whispered in his ear, and he laughed as he handed her the microphone.

"Change of plan, we now have Serena with..."

Serena interrupted him, "Hi, guys. Let's do this before I chicken out."

Taking a deep breath, the opening to..."Baby One More Time" by Brittany Spears started. Serena jumped in singing word for word, not missing a note, and not looking at the monitor; she knew the words by heart. She belted it out and danced across the stage with Brittany, pre-meltdown, pizazz. She shook her hips as she sang. She was having the best time, singing note for note perfectly. Singing alone like this had been something that she had always wanted to do. She loved the thrill of singing with her friends and the funness, but being up there on her own was indescribable. As she sang the last few words, she couldn't help but smile, she was proud that she had done it and could cross it off her bucket list.

When the song finished, she took a bow and everyone went wild. Blake walked towards her and lifted her down off the stage. He spun her around and kissed her, as he pulled back he said, "Holy shit, that was awesome, Serena." He kissed her again. "I knew you could sing, but wow, that was fuckin' out of this world."

"It wasn't that good," she shyly said, as they headed back to the table. A few people on the way back stopped them and congratulated her on her amazing performance.

When they got back to the table, the guys were all staring at her open-mouthed and stunned. Heather was speechless, for the first time ever, and Michele was shaking her head in disbelief. Michele finally spoke up, "Umm, Brittany, where did that come from?"

"My voice box," Serena said as she grabbed her cocktail.

"Hardy har har, bitch. That was forking amazeballs, woman," Heather declared. "You have just put everyone here to shame. How did we not know you could sing like that?"

Serena shrugged her shoulders but didn't say anything further on the subject. "More shots?" she asked everyone, officially taking the attention off her and her singing. She and Blake headed to the bar and ordered another round of shots, but this time they did something different—Blake ordered three Irish Car Bombs for him, Tom, and Robert and three Jäger bombs for the girls.

He looked to Serena. "Tonight's motto is go hard or go home; we are going hard."

She shook her head and mumbled, "Real fucking hard."

While they waited for their drinks, Blake tickled her ribs and she giggled; in that moment, with that one tickle, Serena fell head over heels for him and wished things could be different then they got back to the mainland. They returned to the table and everyone stopped talking, they eyed the drinks as Serena and Blake handed them out.

Robert looked apprehensive, his bravado slipped when he eyed the drinks being handed out. "What the fuck is that?" he asked.

"Irish Car Bombs for us, Jäger bombs for the ladies," Blake said with a grin.

"You are a fucker, you know that?" Robert whined.

"Dude, Heather's words were..." together Serena and Blake chanted, "...Go hard or go home." Blake added, "And we are going hard."

Robert looked at them as he shook his head in disbelief. "Fuck, I knew this would come back to bite me in the ass." Pausing, he looked around the table and everyone was staring at him, he smirked before he conceded, "Fine, you bunch of fuckers, let's do this."

They each grabbed their glass and repeated, "Go hard or go home," and proceeded to chug back their drink. Blake was the first to finish and he slammed his glass down on the table. Heather was next to finish; she licked her lips and smiled. Robert finished next and shook his head, he didn't like that one but he tried to be tough and macho; he swallowed deeply and stared daggers at Blake. Serena was next to finish; she shuddered before doing a little circle dance on the spot. "Uggh," she moaned as she sat back down. Tom and Michele finished at the same time; neither fazed by what they had just drank, but the look that passed between the two of them was electric.

In the blink of an eye, it was just Serena and Blake left at the table; Tom and Michele snuck off together, while Heather and Robert took to the dance floor, but they quickly disappeared. Serena and Blake stared at one another, without saying a word, he entwined his fingers with hers and they headed out of the bar in the direction of the beach, towards 'their spot.'

In silence, they walked along the beach, the only sound was the waves as they crashed on the shore and the light thud from the bar music back at the resort. The moon was full and its light sparkled on the water; it was very romantic...just like the other nights. They got to their spot but rather than sitting on the beach, Serena removed her dress, bra and panties and splashed into the water, diving under to cool her heated skin.

When she resurfaced, Blake was still standing on the beach, staring intently at her in the water. The moonlight revealed that he had stripped off and was buck-naked. Serena raised her hand and with her finger motioned for Blake to come towards her. Ever so slowly, he waded into the water towards her. He was about a meter from her when he stopped. They stood there and stared at one another, the heat radiating off them was scorching, their eyes full of lust, need, want, and desire.

Neither moved a muscle.

Each waited for the other to make the first move.

Serena smirked at Blake.

Blake raised an eyebrow at her in return.

Both stared raptly at one another.

Serena was the first to move; she ran her finger along her stomach and up her chest, circling her perky pink nipples, leaving a burning fire of desire in its wake. A deep growl erupted from Blake's throat; his eyes watched the movement of her finger over her body. His cock was alertly standing to attention. When her hand dipped below the water, he moaned and something in him snapped. He couldn't handle it anymore, he stealthily moved towards her. He gripped her ass and pulled her towards him one swift quick move. His lips crashed against hers in a searing hot kiss. Serena flung her arms around his neck, wrapped her legs around his waist, pressing her breasts against his firm, muscular chest, as she slid down and onto his dick, moaning into his mouth at the intrusion.

They continued to kiss as Blake waded them into deeper water. His hand snaked between them to massage and caress her breasts. She moaned into his mouth and began to grind herself up and down his engorged cock, lost to the sensations coursing through her body. Blake reached down further, and began to rub and circle his finger around her clit. Serena continued to thrust her hips until he was balls-deep inside of her. Serena threw her head back and shoved her tits into his face. Leaning forward he sucked and nipped at her nipples. He kissed his way across her collarbone and up her neck before he covered her mouth with his.

Breaking the kiss, she rested her forehead against his and they stared deep into each other's eyes. They continued to rock back and forth, completely lost in one another. That pleasured, tingly feeling began to gain momentum and before Serena knew it, she was tumbling over the edge. She screamed Blake's name as her orgasm took over her body. Soon after, Blake pulled out, and with a few flicks of his wrist, he unleashed his seed into the ocean.

They both stood there, panting, eyes locked on one another; they were snapped back to reality when a few guys from the shore began shouting. "Fuck yeah, they're getting it on. Fuck her hard."

Serena ducked down under the water in embarrassment, and so she wasn't on display, while Blake spun around, flipping the guys off and yelled, "Fuck off, assholes!"

"Fuck, you!" one of the guys shouted, before his friend pulled on his arm and dragged him again.

"Come on, let's go," he snarled at his friend before he yelled to Blake, "Sorry, dude!"

Blake turned back to Serena and when he looked at her, she burst out laughing. "Oh My God...how much do you think they saw? I was so lost in the moment that everything around us disappeared," she said in between fits of giggles. "Man, Heather is going to lose her shit when I tell her about this. On this trip I have managed a striptease and a live sex show; fuck my life."

Blake pulled her into his arms and hugged her as he gently kissed her temple. "No idea, how much they saw, babe, but I don't think they would have seen too much, more just heard what was happening. I was covering you and the moon went behind the clouds so I think we were safe...ish." Pausing, he then added, "And I can say, without a doubt, best striptease I have ever seen." He winked at her. "And the sex show, well..."

Serena laughed as she shoved Blake in the chest. "On

both accounts, I'm glad it was you." She tightened her arms around him and rested her head on his shoulder. Shaking her head, she began to laugh again. "Heather will totally get a kick out of this."

"Hey, I'm getting a kick out of this AND I got to see you naked," Blake said on a laugh. "Well, that's four of six being busted, let's see if Michele and Tom can make it six for six, in the next twenty-four hours."

Serena pursed her lips at him. "Yeah, nah, totally not gonna happen. There is no way in hell Michele will do anything in public."

"Umm, Heather and Rob weren't in public."

"Touché'. Anything is possible then." Serena snuggled into him and shivered.

"You're freezing. Let's head back and warm you up."

"How are you planning on warming me up?" Serena seductively asked, as she wiggled her eyebrows suggestively.

"Wouldn't you like to know?" Blake said as he pinched her nipple. Serena pushed away from him and splashed. A water fight broke out until Serena launched herself at Blake, taking him underwater with her. While under the water, Serena pulled him towards her and kissed him. By then, they were kneeling and close to the shore. Serena pushed Blake back into the sand and straddled him. Lying on top of him, she kissed and nibbled his neck, up and along his jawline before her lips crashed to his. Their lips fused together in a heat-filled kiss, Blake held Serena close to him as they lost themselves in the act. In one swift motion, he flipped them over so she was suddenly under him, he cocooned her with his arms and they stared deeply into each other's eyes. He kissed down her neck and chest; his hand began massaging her breasts, rolling her nipple between his forefinger and thumb. Squeezing the tip before sucking it deep into his mouth. Serena moaned as she ran her fingers through his blond locks. Blake pulled back and looked intently at Serena. "Do you want me to fuck you here in the sand? Or do you want to go back to the room with less sand?"

Serena whispered "Both," She began to rub her pussy on his leg and pulled him in for another kiss. She spread her legs and invited him in. He rolled his hips and effortlessly slid inside her wet channel. "Fuck me, you're so wet."

"Shut up and fuck me," Serena growled as she crashed her lips to his, widening her legs to let him in deeper. Through their kiss she heard him moan in agreement. She raked her fingers down his back and squeezed his ass tightly, before she wrapped her legs around him and pulled him in closer. Like a well-oiled machine, they thrust back and forth until they were both tumbling over the edge, shouting each other's names. The earth-shattering explosion of her orgasm detonated, invoking the most intense toe-curling orgasm of her life; this one was off the Richter scale shattering.

Completely drained, Serena's arm fell back to the sand, she lay there staring up at Blake, panting and smiling. "What are you smiling at?" Blake murmured.

"That was, just, umm, yeah, wow. I don't want to go home tomorrow."

Blake climbed off Serena and pulled her into a sitting position, her back to his front; he wrapped his arms around her and whispered into her ear, "Serena, this has been the best week of my life." Pausing, he hesitantly added, "I want to see you when we get back."

"Not this again Blake, please." She paused and began

to rub Blake's arm, looking over her shoulder she whispered, "Let's keep what we have in Oasis, and leave with amazing memories of one another."

Blake sighed in frustration as he stared out at the ocean, the darkness mirroring his current emotion. He didn't want this to end, but at the same time he didn't want to pressure her. He kissed her temple again but didn't answer her. "Let's head back." Blake stood up and put a hand out to help Serena up, she took his hand and they headed over to their clothes. Silently they got dressed and walked back along the beach towards Oasis, hand in hand; both of them lost in their thoughts.

CHAPTER 18

THE ATMOSPHERE AT BREAKFAST THE NEXT MORNING WAS FULL of tension, unease, and sadness…until Robert and Heather joined them. You could always count on those two to provide laughs, and it was just what everyone needed.

The shuttle back to the airport was due to leave at 11:00 a.m. so they all decided that one last ocean swim was called for. The six of them walked towards the beach, laughing and joking, when Robert said, "Did you hear, there were two people porking out here last night?"

Blake smirked and glanced towards Serena, her face turning red at where the conversation was headed. He could tell, by the look in her eyes, she was remembering their beach escapades from last night and how amazingly awesome it was.

Tom looked to Robert. "Who says porking these days?"

"Okay, bumping uglies, fucking, gettin' it on, screwing..."

"We get it, Robert," Michele butted in. She looked towards Serena and offered a shy smile, knowing it was her 'porking' last night.

Heather, being Heather, looked to Serena and with a grin said, "Serena, you're pretty quiet, and your face tells me it was you and Blake bumping uglies out here last night."

Serena's mouth dropped open, Heather totally just dumped her in it; some friend she was. "Ummm," Serena murmured, her face was quickly beetroot red and her neck blotching with embarrassment, but she was unable to hide her grin. The memories of last night came crashing back to her, and she not so quietly moaned, clenching her thighs together and bit her lip.

In unison, Michele and Heather shouted, "Remembergasm!"

At that point, Serena's face was redder than a lobster and Robert didn't help the situation when he turned to Blake and shouted, "You dirty fucking dawg!" Offering up his hand for a high five; Blake didn't high five him back. He stared at Serena sadly and sighed. Yes, last night was beyond amazing, but it would all end in a few hours...he was not ready to let go of her yet. She could feel his stare boring into her, and it only magnified how shitty she felt about shutting him down last night. She confided in Michele that morning that she thought she made the wrong decision. She'd love nothing more than to continue this with Blake when they got back, BUT she was scared and too proud to admit to him that she might have made a mistake...leaving with the memories from Oasis would have to do.

Michele, being the great friend that she was, ripped her sundress over her head and raced towards the water shouting, "Last one in is a rotten egg!" That snapped everyone to attention and clothes were stripped off left, right, and center. They all sprinted towards the water; that was everyone except Blake.

Serena hit the waterline and from the corner of her eye noticed that Blake was just standing there, holding his shirt in his hand, not moving. She spun on her heel and walked over to him. "You coming?"

"Yeah, just gimme a minute." He turned his back on her and that movement cut her deeply. He slowly walked towards the palm trees and took a seat in the sand. He stared out to sea, his shoulder slumped in sadness; Serena knew it was because of her. She followed him and squatted down in front of him, she rested her palms on his knees, looked up at him and asked, "Blake, talk to me, what's up?"

"It's nothing, Serena." She looked at him, her eyes implored him to spill his guts. "It's just, I don't want to go home today 'cause it means I won't be seeing you anymore." He looked down at his feet, not bearing to look at her.

"I'm sorry," Serena whispered, as she fell to her knees in front of him, a lone tear slipped out of her eye and cascaded down her cheek. Blake lifted his hand and with the pad of his thumb gently wiped the tear away. "Blake, I'll miss you too, but as I've previously said, I just can't right now."

"I know, it just fucking sucks," he replied. He under-stood where she was coming from, and he accepted her decision, it just sucked donkey balls because he had fallen hard for Serena Bateman.

"We still have," Serena looked at her watch, "Three hours and forty-two minutes left at Oasis. Let's enjoy it while we can." Blake looked at her and smiled; it amazed him at how easily she could calm him and bring him back to reality. He leaned forward and placed a gentle kiss on the tip of her nose and gazed into her eyes. Without warning, he jumped up, threw Serena over his shoulder, and made a run for the ocean. When the water was thigh-high, he threw her high into the air; she crashed into the water with a splash.

Her subsequent scream paused the current water fight, all eyes currently on her and Blake. Finally she surfaced, coughing and spluttering, everyone, except Serena began laughing.

"Ohh, it's on like Donkey Kong, asshole," Serena declared, jumping up and lunging for Blake, but he was too quick. He stepped to the side and she crashed into the water next to him. He reached out and grabbed Serena, pulling her to him and wrapped his arms tightly around her. He spun her around and kissed her deeply.

The others began splashing the couple while making kissing sounds, Tom singing, "Bum Chicka Wow Wow."

Robert yelled, "Get a room, fuckers!"

Serena broke the kiss and looked over to Robert, "Rob, get fucked, this is our beach." She winked at him with a smirk before she turned her attention back to Blake and resumed their searing kiss...on what was now, and would forever be known as 'their' beach.

Everyone laughed, Robert flipped her the bird and then proceeded to tackle Heather into the water. Taking her by surprise, she screamed at the unexpected takedown.

Serena and Blake broke their lips and looked to them in the water and laughed.

Blake turned his attention back to Serena, he gripped her cheeks and kissed her deeply again. Finally they broke apart, Serena was left breathless and lightheaded; that was one earth-shattering kiss and one that she'd remember forever. She quickly tried to dunk Blake but he was too quick for her. He grabbed her wrist and tugged her backwards; they both tumbled under the water.

After their impromptu swim, they all headed back to the beach, and lazed in the morning sun for the last time. Soon, it was time to pack, but the last few hours at Oasis were fun-filled, with many laughs, but also fraught with unhappiness at the impending departure and imminent goodbyes.

CHAPTER 19

AFTER CHECKING OUT, THE SIX OF THEM SILENTLY BOARDED the shuttle for the airport; amazingly it was just them on the bus. The atmosphere was quiet and subdued; the fun and laughs from earlier gone, replaced with sadness, deep thoughts, and longing as they realised they were heading back to reality.

They had checked in for the return flight and luck was on their side, they managed to snag seats together and an upgrade to premium economy. While waiting for the plane, they headed to the Castaway Grove airport bar, even though the airport was a tin shed, it had one amaze-balls bar. Robert and Heather offered to get drinks. Because it was quiet today, they got served pretty quickly and ordered beers and snacks for everyone.

Once everyone had his or her drinks, Tom cleared his throat. "A toast. To what has been an amazing week." In unison, they all raised their glasses and said a mixture of "Cheers," "Amen." And from Robert, "Fuck yeah." Robert's eloquently put declaration caused them to all laugh and as usual, Robert managed to ease the atmosphere and turn the sadness around. Just like it had been for the last seven days, the six of them fell into their usual banter, full of fun and laughs.

A few rounds later, their flight was called. They finished their drinks, collected their carry-on items, and lined up for their journey back to reality. With that announcement, the air changed once again, and the six of them reflected…

…Robert was excited to be getting back. as he missed his dogs and he was eager to start at his dad's advertising company as an ad executive.

…Heather was excited to get back to reality, as she would be going from trainee at the medical center to a full-fledged nurse…and she missed her puppy, too.

…Tom was happy to have Michele in his life and to get to know her on a deeper level, back on the mainland; he had fallen head over heels for her…and she had fallen for him, too.

…Michele was looking forward to starting full-time work, even if it was just as a personal assistant. If all went well, it would lead to an executive PA position within the law firm…and to get to know Tom further.

…Blake was excited for the job change at his work to be finalised. He just wished they would hurry up and make a decision, because living in limbo was hard; he was also sad to be leaving Serena.

...Serena was excited to start her first real job as an adult, and to finally live on her own. She was over dorm living and college life, she was ready for adulthood; she was also upset and questioning her decision in regards to Blake.

The plane trip itself was uneventful, as you would hope when you fly. While they waited for their luggage, they reminisced about the past week at Oasis; they all laughed at the pact that the girls made...which was broken before the plane had even departed. Through laughter, Heather stated, "I can't believe that we didn't even make it twenty-four hours before our 'no boys' rule was null and void."

Michele added, "We didn't even last eight minutes. We were all smitten, in one way or another, while waiting in the departure lounge." Everyone nodded in agreement.

Robert wrapped his arms around Heather's waist and cockily stated, "Well, the three of us are pretty hard to resist." He nuzzled her neck as he said that. She spun around in his arms and they proceeded to make out in the middle of baggage claim.

Michele and Serena shook their head at them. "Get a room!" Serena yelled.

Robert broke the kiss with Heather, flipped her the bird, and cheekily replied, "To quote a wise woman, 'get fucked', Serena." He winked before turning his attention back to Heather; he dipped her back in an over-the-top romantic kiss. He placed Heather back to her feet, her cheeks were flushed with embarrassment...but Serena had never seen her friend look happier.

The luggage was finally delivered and once they each

had their suitcases, they made their way towards the exit. Everyone hugged and said their goodbyes.

Blake grabbed Serena's hand and pulled her to the side. "Serena, please take my number. I don't expect you to call right away, as I know your life is going to be crazy, but for the future…please."

Serena looked at him, his eyes are pleading with her. "Blake, as much as I want to, I can't, we've discussed this. I know I'm being a bitch, only thinking of myself, but I need to start this next chapter on my own." She wiped away a stray tear. "I'm sorry."

In an act of desperation, he pulled her towards him, held her cheeks between his palms and whispered, "You are not a bitch, Serena. You are a phenomenal woman." He then placed his lips gently against her. His tongue traced along her lips before he slipped it inside her mouth. He kissed her deeply, dipping her back in his arms, just like they did in the movies. Both of them were lost in their final searing kiss, they were oblivious to the people moving about around them. Everyone else faded away, it was just the two of them and their final goodbye.

Blake placed Serena back on her feet, her heart thumping rapidly in her chest cavity, her breathing laboured, her cheeks pink with lust, and her lips tingling from the single most romantic emotion-filled kiss of her life. "Goodbye, Serena," he whispered, placing a gentle kiss on her cheek before turning around and walking away.

Serena stood there, holding her cheek where his lips just were, and she watched him walk away and exit the airport. When the airport doors closed, the first tear fell and her heart broke into a million tiny pieces. "Closing

Time" by Semisonic began playing and the tears then poured down her face. Heather and Michele wrapped her in a group hug, and through her sobs she blubbered, "I think I made a mistake."

CHAPTER 20

SERENA HAD BEEN BACK FROM OASIS FOR SEVEN WEEKS AND had settled into real life and adulthood quite well. Her new job was amazing and she was really enjoying it, much more than she thought she would. The last box had finally been unpacked, and she was all settled into her new apartment; she absolutely loved living on her own. At times, she did miss dorm living, but mostly she missed having Michele and Heather with her all the time. The only thing that would have made everything perfect at the moment would be having Blake in her life.

She thought it would be easy to just have a fling and leave with the memories, but she didn't count on falling head over heels in love with Blake so quickly. Serena constantly kicked herself, not only did she tell him that it was only a holiday fling, but she refused his number at the airport; dumbest decision ever made by Serena Bateman. If she wasn't too proud, she knew she could ask the girls to get his number, but her pride is preventing her from doing so. It seemed that what happened in Oasis would stay at Oasis.

It was Friday and Serena would be meeting up with Heather and Michele for a night of cocktails and dancing; it had become a weekly tradition since returning. She knew, without a doubt, that they would pull her out of her funk, even if just for the night. Due to a last minute printing issue, she was late leaving the office. As she exited the building, she dug in her bag for her phone to text the girls that that she was on her way, when she bumped into someone; she stumbled and dropped her phone. An arm reached out to steady her before they bent down to pick her phone up for her. He was down on one knee in front of her, with her phone is his hand, and he looked up at her.

They both gasped in shock. In unison they each said the other's name.

"Serena!"

"Blake!"

They both stood in the middle of the sidewalk, staring at each other, not caring that they were blocking the path. All those feelings from Oasis came rushing back to Serena, her heart rate sped up and her face broke out into the biggest smile. "Whh...what? How? Whhh...why are you here?" Serena stammered.

"I live in the city now," he replied. He smiled at her like he did eight weeks ago on the plane and all the memories and happy times came flooding like a bolt of lightning to her heart.

Serena shivered as she remembered. "Yes, but here, here?"

"I work here now." He pointed to the building across the street. "My up in the air job was finally finalised. I moved to the city and I started here earlier this week."

"No fucking way?" she excitedly replied.

"Yes, fucking way," he said with a smirk.

"I work there." Serena nodded towards the building beside them. She was still grinning and staring at Blake; not quite believing that he was there, in front of her. Serena's eyes were locked on his, she kept waiting for him to disappear or for her to wake up. Her eyes roamed over his body and she stifled a moan as memories of Oasis flashed before her. She thought he looked hot in boardies, but all decked out in a suit and tie, holy hotness, Batman. For a woman, a man in a suit and tie was what a woman in lingerie was to a man, and Blake wore the shit out of his suit.

"Eyes up here, gorgeous," Blake said, those words vibrated through Serena and she clenches her thighs together.

"Sorry, I just can't believe you're here...in front of me."

"Serena, I saw you exit the building. My eyes were locked on you, I was sure that my eyes were playing tricks on me, and then you were in front of me. I've been miserable these past seven weeks. Not seeing you was much harder than I thought possible. Not throwing my number at you was the dumbest thing I have ever done. SO many times, I wanted to get your number from Michele or Heather, but I knew they wouldn't have given it up."

"Blake, I've wanted to get your number from the guys ever since we got back too, but I let my pride get in the way. Not getting your number was the second most stupidest thing I have ever done. The first was not giving us a chance." Pausing, she looked up at him and shyly asked, "Umm, Blake, do you wanna grab a drink?"

"I'd love nothing more, Serena," he eagerly replied.

Biting her lip to suppress a smile, they linked their fingers together and silently walked towards the bar on the corner; blissfully happy to be reunited...maybe what happens in Oasis doesn't stay at Oasis after all!

The End!!!!

Unequivocal Love

I'd never believed in love at first sigh...then I met her, Hartley Bannon.
She is my true love.
My soul mate.
My end game.
I thought nothing could tear us apart.
Until I proposed.
My beautiful, caring, fun loving, sexy as hell fiancée is now possessed by Bridezilla. And she's threatening to rip our happily ever after to shreds and destroy everything we worked so hard to achieve.
The only thing keeping me together is the mind blowing make up sex after every fight, but what if that isn't enough? Is my love for her strong enough to defeat Bridezilla? or is this the beginning of the end for us?

PAIGE

He said five words I never thought he would say to me. Those five words ripped my heart from my chest and obliterated me.

Needing time to myself, I head to a beach resort to clear my head, to find myself. I realize staying away isn't what I want.

I want him to want me.

Five words sent me away, but are there any words that will help me walk back?

———

CAM

I regretted the words as soon as they were out of my mouth, but it was too late. She was already walking away.

The time apart makes me realize I want her in my life. I don't want to be alone. Sending her away isn't what I want.

I want her back.

Five words caused her to walk away, but are there any words to get her to walk back?

Rule #1: Never fall in love.
Rule #2: Never sleep with a local.
Rule #3: Never sleep with the same person twice
Rule #4: No glove, no love.
Rule #5: Never break Rules 1-4.

These are the rules that I've lived by since I opened The Grove Bar three years ago, but in the last thirty-six hours, I have broken most of them…repeatedly. And boy-oh-boy, did I break them.

Damn you, Burton-f'ing-Hayes.

I didn't just break my rules with this sexy as sin man; I smashed every one of them to smithereens, and then set each one on fire and pissed on the simmering ashes.

Life was easy with my rules, but now that I've obliterated them, I don't know what to do. Do I follow my heart and set new rules? Or do I stick to my original rules and risk it all?

They say rules are meant to be broken, but at what cost?

OASIS PLAYLIST

Wild Ones – Flo Rida feat, Sia
Breathe – The Prodigy
Big Jet Plane – Angus & Julia Stone
Girls Just Wanna Have Fun – Cyndi Lauper
Whip It – DEVO
You Keep Me Hangin On – Kim Wild
Bye Bye Bye - *NYSYNC
Everybody (Backstreet's Back) – Backstreet Boys
It's Alright – East 17
Take On Me – a-ha
Alive – Natalie Bassingthwaighte
Voodoo Child – Rogue Traders
Crazy – Seal
American Pie – Don McClean
Papa Don't Preach – Kelly Osbourne
Mustang Sally – The Commitments
Wannaba – Spice Girls
I Will Survive – Gloria Gaynor
Baby Got Back – Sir Mix-A-Lot
Kokomo – The Beach Boys

Redneck Woman – Gretchen Wilson
Livin' On A Prayer – Bon Jovi
We Are The Champions – Queen
All of Me – John Legend
See You Again – Wiz Khalifa feat. Charlie Puth
Before He Cheats – Carrie Underwood
...Baby One More Time – Brittany Spears
You Give Love A Bad Name - Bon Jovi
Closing Time – Semisonic
All I Wanna Do – Sheryl Crow

This playlist can be found on spotify.

ACKNOWLEDGMENTS

Michele and Heather, your friendship was the inspiration behind these characters and our love of **Nick, Tom** and **Robert** was a added bonus to this story. Even though we have never met, it feels like I have known you both forever. I forking love you guys and cannot wait till we meet in person.

My hubby, **Troy,** and my munchkins, **Piper** and **Kade**; you three are my biggest supporters. Your encouragement, support and patience are muchly appreciated, I could not do this without you guys. Love you long-time family XoXoX

To my beta's **Beth, Amanda, Crissy, Megan** and **Michelle**. Thank you for taking the time to read this. It so different to what I have previously written and I doubted myself with every word that I wrote. Your feedback was greatly appreciated.

My wonderful editor, **Karen** from Barren Acres Editing.

I've finally written the style of book you thought I would write but I must tell you, the next one will be a suspense again cause the RomCom if hard work, give me murder, beatings, suspense and intrigue any day. Thank you for dotting my I's and crossing my T's; you truly are wonderful at what you do.

Tash Drake, thank you for making my stunning cover and teasers. As soon as I saw it I had to have it and your awesome cover inspired this story and the teasers match perfectly.

And last but not least, **my readers.** Without you guys taking a chance on lil old me, I wouldn't be releasing my fourth book. Thank you for your support and reviews, I really really appreciate it.

ALSO BY DL GALLIE

STAND ALONES

Out of Nowhere

Antecedent

Seven Nights

Doc Steel

Summer Heat

The Rule Breaker anthology

In the Dark of Night anthology

Love is Contagious, a charity anthology

———

THE CASTAWAY GROVE COLLECTION

Love has arrived in the Grove

Oasis

Unequivocal Love

Five Words

Broken Rules - coming late 2020

…and a few more as well.

———

FALLING NOVELS

Falling for Dr. Kelly

Falling for Dr. Knight

Falling for Agent Cox - coming late 2020

―――

THE LIQUOR CABINET SERIES

Liquor has never been so disturbingly saucy

Malt Me (Book 1)

Tequila Healing (Book 2)

Wine Not (Book 3)

The Final Shot (Book 4)

The Liquor Cabinet: Series boxset

―――

THE UNEXPECTED SERIES

When it comes to love, expect the unexpected

The Unexpected Gift

The Unexpected Letter

The Unexpected Package

The Unexpected Connection

CONTACT THE AUTHOR

FACEBOOK ~ INSTAGRAM ~ BOOKBUB

GOODREADS ~ WEBSITE

dlgallieauthor@outlook.com

Sign up to my newsletter

ABOUT THE AUTHOR

DL Gallie is from Queensland, Australia, but she's lived in many different places all over the world, including the UK and Canada. She currently resides in Central Queensland with her husband and two munchkins. She and her husband have been together  since she was sixteen, and although they drive each other crazy at times, she couldn't imagine her life without him.

Shortly after her son was born, DL began reading again. With encouragement from her husband, she picked up the pen and started writing, and now the voices in her head won't shut up.

DL enjoys listening to music, drinking white wine in the summer, red wine in the winter, and beer all year round. She's also never been known to turn down a cocktail, especially a margarita.

www.ingramcontent.com/pod-product-compliance
Lightning Source LLC
Chambersburg PA
CBHW020621120726
47905CB00003B/881